GERALDINE MOORKENS BYRNE

The Music Shop Mysteries

First edition

ISBN: 978-1-7396496-1-6

This book was professionally typeset on Reedsy.
Find out more at reedsy.com

Dedicated to the memory of
Charles Byrne
1931 - 2022

and
Charles Byrne Music Shop,
Stephen Street Lower, Dublin
1870 - 2021

Contents

Preface

Charles Byrne Music, 1870 - 2021

This book has been a labour of love.

From 1870 until 2021, my family owned a music shop in Stephen Street Lower, in Dublin. It became Ireland's oldest family-owned music shop, and throughout its long history, my family became part of the cultural and social fabric of the city.

For thirty years, I had the privilege of working in and finally running the shop. If we were to write half the real stories that occurred, no one would believe us. But while we were never called upon to investigate a murder, this story is packed with echoes of the real musicians, characters, trials and triumphs of our history.

Our city remains a powerful mix of new and old, a modern capital steeped in history and proud of its heritage. It is also enriched by new people, and fresh outlooks. If you ever get to visit, I highly recommend the area around the fictional "West Stephen Street," which may be found in real life in Lower Stephen Street, South William Street, Drury Street and the many fabulous independent creatives and retailers that find a home there.

The music mentioned in this book is real - if you check out the Irish traditional music listed, you can find them all online. Except *The Sandymount Reel*, which I invented - in its stead, check out *The Marino Waltz*, by the great player, composer, and poet, John Sheehan.

And while no one character is directly lifted from real life, the main cast are inspired by the many lovely customers, and friends, that graced the doors of our shop.

Mrs. O'Brien is directly inspired by my mother, but don't tell her. She'll only get a big head.

The character made her debut in a bestselling charity anthology in 2023, The Little Shop of Murders, which raised funds for children's charities across Ireland, Uk and USA.

Neapolitan Luigi Salzedo Mandolin, 1890

Cast of Characters
O'Brien's Music Shop
Mrs. Teresa O'Brien, Proprietor
Mr. Michael Clancy, Luthier
West Stephen Street
Mr. and Mrs. Khan, Mai Khan - The Noodle Palace
Paddy - The Bald Bear Barbers
Ashmara Kapoor, Setanta Kapoor - Kapoors Vintage and Fashion Emporium
Denise, Dan - Fancies Cafe
The Super Ukers
Clara and Peadair
Catherine
Eamonn

And
Eugene Brook, Liam Pollard -Brook and Pollard Ltd, Com-

mercial Property Experts
   Annmarie Pollard
   Councillor Michelle Costello
   Councillor Seamus Molloy
   Finbar O'Leary, Mandolinist

GLOSSARY

   Eejit = a soft or foolish person
   Garda (singular) Gardaí (plural) - Irish Police
   Gom - an easily led, foolish person
   G'won - the Dublin way to say "Go On."
   G'won outta that - "No way," or "Give over."
   Uilleann Pipes - the Irish pipes, literally "pipes of the elbow,"
as they are inflated by the action of the arm at the elbow rather
than blown into.

Acknowledgement

As ever, grateful thanks to the Beta readers, whose feedback is invaluable.

With gratitude to the many loyal customers and friends of the real life version of "O'Brien's Music Shop," - you made it a pleasure.

Especial thanks to Fran Crowther, of DublinTown.ie whose help and support over the years, I will always appreciate.

Chapter 1

Mrs. O'Brien looked around the tiny music shop and was satisfied. The glass showcases were full, every stand and hook boasting a musical instrument – Violins, a few Cellos, Ukuleles, Mandolins, in all sizes and with an array of gleaming woods and varnish. As well as the instruments, every nook and cranny of the old place was stuffed with as many accessories, gig bags, music stands, strings that a musician could desire. There were Bodhráns, the Irish drum, hanging from the ceiling and a display of silver and brass traditional Irish whistles from high D to Low D. Not only could the eye feast on this array of musical stock, but the ear was also tickled by the gentle echo of the instruments as they reverberated to every movement inside and sometimes, outside, the shop.

The building was large enough; three stories with two rooms each, with thick walls built in the last years of the eighteenth century. On the top floor were storerooms, housing whatever stock couldn't fit into the retail section on the ground floor. It was packed full, extra Double basses, cellos and guitars taking up more space than the shop floor could spare. On the middle floor were the workrooms, where old Mr. O'Brien had worked from the age of thirteen to his death the previous year. Now they were the pride and joy of Michael Clancy, the young Luthier who had taken over the repair and restoration business. He was a cheerful, hardworking young man and he loved instruments as if they were living creatures. Mr. O'Brien would have approved.

On the ground floor the front room was given over to the retail shop, with the back room being the office. That was where she did her accounts, made lunch for Michael and herself, and when time permitted surfed the web and browsed social media. At almost eighty, she prided herself on keeping up to date with everything including technology. Helped by her granddaughter Christina she had set up an Instant-photo account where she posted pictures of all her precious stock – it had gained quite the cult following. She took several photos of her newly organized showcases with her mobile phone, ready to upload later that day.

But first, she promised herself a nice cup of coffee and maybe a small bun. Her sweet tooth was her Achilles heel, and the honey cakes the neighbouring café made were to die for. It was half past two, she had missed her lunch unpacking the latest consignment of ukuleles. Surely she deserved a little afternoon pick-me-up?

Michael was hard at work upstairs, so she grabbed her keys, clipped the shop door shut and popped into the building next to her. When she had first married, and began working with her husband Cathal, West Stephen Street had been a hive of small shops. A butcher's, a men's clothes shop, a bakery and a shoe shop, along with a newsagent slash sweet shop that sold everything from cigarette papers to yo-yos. Over five decades the street had changed – new apartments and a car park had taken away many of the old shops, but in their stead was an array of new, modern businesses. A coffee shop, two restaurants, a barber, a website developer and a shop selling handmade Irish gifts all changed the atmosphere to one of vibrancy and youth. She missed the old days but enjoyed the colour and energy of the area now.

"Everything must change," Mrs. O'Brien liked to say, "But in the end, it's people who matter!" And the people surrounding her little music shop now were as good, kind and hardworking as their predecessors.

Mr. Khan from the Noodle Palace brought over a lunch to her several times, when her husband died, and she was all alone trying to keep the business open. It was her first time eating Duck Noodles with Mr. Khan's Special Sauce and she had enjoyed it, even if she had had to drink half a litre of milk for the heat. Mr. Khan's special sauce was powerful stuff. The young fella who ran the posh hairdressers had bought a tray of sticky cakes from her grandson Fintan when he was fundraising for his Hurling club. She was sure badly decorated cupcakes didn't fit in with the aesthetic of The Bald Bear Barbers but Paddy Lynch, the owner, had made young Fintan feel like a professional baker. Mrs. Kapoor, whose hipster clothes emporium was frequently mentioned in the Irish Gazette "Lifestyle" section, had taken in two huge boxes of instruments while Mrs. O'Brien was out sick and unable to open. They sat in the Kapoor's shop, taking up space and making life difficult, until she returned to work. Then Setanta Kapoor, the owner's son, had carried them down, opened them up and helped her display them.

Up and down the little street, behind every window display

and trendy décor, a dozen tales of little kindnesses lay ready to be told. Mrs. O'Brien often remarked how lucky she was to be surrounded by such nice neighbours, without realizing that her neighbours said the same thing about her. She had spent a lifetime sowing a garden of kindness and now in her later years, she was seeing it bloom.

Mindful of the time, and not wanting to miss a potential customer while the shop was unattended, she slipped into *Fancies*, Dublin's finest coffee shop. She liked a nice cup of tea, but since discovering the lattes in Fancies, she had developed quite the habit for mid-afternoon coffee with a choice of delicate pastry or scrumptious cake. The current favourite was honey cake, which combined sweetness with melt-in-your-mouth lightness and really felt like you hadn't actually indulged at all.

Denise, one of the two owners, smiled at her. "Your usual, Mrs. O'Brien?"

"Teresa, please. And yes, a latte and um, let's see...ah sure, a honey cake."

"Still on them. are you? You'll have to try our cheesecakes next. But between us, those honey cakes are my favourite too. I keep eating them!" She patted her waistline and grinned. "I'll have to cut back!"

"Nonsense. You've a lovely figure," Teresa O'Brien replied truthfully. Denise was in her late forties, always nicely turned out, and carried herself very well. "And believe me, when you reach my age you won't *ever* say "I wish I hadn't eaten that nice thing.""

Denise laughed. "My granny used to tell us, you'll only regret the things you *didn't* do!"

"That's the truth! So, where's Daniel today?"

Denise's business partner was usually to be found behind the counter, while she preferred the role of admin and accountant. It was a rare day when he wasn't cracking jokes and exchanging pleasantries with the customers. They were best friends, although from the way Denise looked at him, she wouldn't mind being more.

"Oh, don't ask! He's off meeting with the landlord. You know that group that bought over the building?"

The coffee shop, Mrs. Kapoor's boutique Hipster Heaven, and The Bald Bear Barbers were on the ground floor of a building with four stories of apartments above them. Until very recently, the entire building had been owned by a company called Dublin Holdings Ltd. Recently however, the situation had changed, much to everyone's dismay. Southside Developments had bought out Dublin Holdings Ltd. No one knew much about them, except that it was Irish owned. The sale had gone through without the tenants even knowing it was on the cards. It wouldn't have mattered so much if everything had continued in the established way but the new owners had written to each tenant, including those in the apartments above, warning of rent hikes. They demanded a meeting with each business owner, to discuss new terms and conditions and so far had ignored any inquiries or questions outside of that, making everyone involved worried and on edge.

"You're so lucky, Teresa. You own your premises. It's so hard to rent nowadays. Commercial rent is ridiculous in this area as it is. What on earth will we do if they raise the rent?" Denise blinked, a suspicion of tears in her blue eyes. "Mrs. Kapoor says she will definitely have to move once her lease is up. She'll probably go completely online, not that she wants to but at least it's an option. Can't sell coffee and cakes online."

"Oh, I *am* sorry. But surely they can't just raise them? You have a tenancy agreement."

"I don't think they can do it to the domestic tenants, but once our lease is up next year, they can renegotiate."

Teresa shook her head. "That's a disgrace, the country on its knees and small businesses being squeezed like that."

"Look at the arcade around the corner - their landlord froze all rents during the pandemic. Couldn't have been kinder."

"Absolutely. I wish I could suggest something, but I don't know anything about tenants' rights. Have you taken legal advice?"

"Daniel is meeting with someone tomorrow. He's going to listen to what the landlord says today and take notes."

"Good for him. I bet ye have more rights than you think - these corporate types think they can bully people. What about the council? Wasn't your man on about small businesses the other day? Whatshisname, Seamus something."

"Councillor Seamus Molloy." Denise shook her head sourly. "He's worse than useless. Don't believe a word he says in front of the cameras. He's a landlord himself. Owns a lot of buildings around here, and he's as twisty as a pig's tail."

"Oh dear. Well, they can't all be corrupt. Maybe get in touch with other councilors."

"Maybe. Anyway, I'm sorry for unloading on you - you only came in for a coffee and I bent your ear about our problems!"

"Don't be daft, Denise. I am happy to listen. I'm not much use to you, I'm afraid, but I'm good at listening."

Mrs. O'Brien took her leave, sighing as she let herself back into the old music shop. She unclipped the door and turned the sign to "open" before wandering into the office and sipping her coffee. The honey cake was divine, but it didn't lift her mood quite as much as it would usually. Denise and Daniel, and her other business neighbours, deserved better than a greedy landlord forcing them out.

A clatter of noise on the stairs told her that Michael had emerged from his workrooms and was making his way downstairs. He was a tall, gangly young man who looked as if he'd been put together out of elbows and knees. He was attractive rather than handsome; a warm and friendly face, with laughter lines already embedded around his eyes and mouth, and a shock of unruly dark hair. She smiled as he appeared in the doorway, clutching a mandolin, his face bright with excitement.

"I think I've fixed it!" He held the instrument aloft as if it was a trophy. "No more buzz!"

The mandolin had been left in by a despairing musician, the famous Finbar O'Leary.

"I can't stand it," Finbar had wailed, handing it to Michael to examine. "It's my favourite. I love this mandolin so much!"

"What's the problem?" Michael had asked. The instrument was a handmade Hofner, German made, with a tone that was perfect for Irish traditional music.

"It buzzes. Out of nowhere - one minute it was fine and the next, a buzz between the fifth and ninth frets."

He swore he hadn't dropped it, left it in direct sunlight or propped it up against a hot radiator. Michael suspected that something untoward had happened, but O'Leary was a good customer and an experienced player. It was unlikely he had damaged it. Maybe someone else had knocked it, unbeknownst to him. Accidents happened on stage or in the studio all the time.

A few days of painstaking work, readjusting the neck and settling frets, had paid off.

"I genuinely thought it would never stop buzzing," the young man said. "Listen!"

He played up and down the fingerboard, Mrs. O'Brien listening intently.

"Not a hint of a buzz," she agreed. "Well done."

"It was annoying me. I'll give it a day to be sure, but if it's really gone, he can collect it tomorrow. How's it going down here? Any news?"

"Quiet enough," Mrs. O'Brien replied. "To be honest, I've been more concerned with what's happening next door."
"The new landlords? Has anyone met with them yet?"

"Daniel is meeting them today. Denise is really worried about it. She was telling me how difficult they are to deal with. And she's worried about the rent going up."

"It's a disgrace. If they push out the business tenants, who do they think will afford the higher rent? Small businesses are only clinging on as it is, in the city centre."

"It's very short-sighted, I agree. Perhaps the tenants can put a financial argument forward - I assume the new owners want to make money, not have empty units gathering dust."
"I wouldn't be so sure. Lots of buildings are left empty and written off against tax. That journalist, the one with the posh accent and the big hair - she did a segment on it on Prime News recently."

"Philomena Quinn, and I saw it. But it was a fully empty building, not ones with domestic tenants in apartments. Perhaps an accountant could advise them?"

"Or a lawyer," Michael replied. "I'd get a solicitor on the case."

Mrs. O'Brien nodded. If Daniel's meeting had gone badly, then all the tenants would need professional advice.
"He has one on standby, Denise said. I'll pop in tomorrow and

see if there's any developments."

* * *

Denise looked up from the cake counter, where she was arranging the newly baked goodies, and Mrs. O'Brien immediately guessed the news wasn't good. The younger woman looked like she had had a bad night's sleep, and there was a defeated slump to her shoulders.

"Should I ask? Or was it a disaster?"

"Awful! Poor Dan is in bits. The man representing the new owners wouldn't even listen to him. Just said that the rent was going up, and we could take it or leave it."

"I'm so sorry. Michael and I were talking about it yesterday. I know you have a lawyer lined up, but we were wondering if there was any case to be made that they can't get higher rents around here? These are small enough units, and small businesses can't afford huge rents."

"The rep was so unreasonable, I doubt he would listen. But may if we could bypass him and talk directly to the company - it's worth trying."

"Maybe the guy you're dealing with is only a lackey," Mrs. O'Brien suggested. "Sometimes these types overstep and try to make a name for themselves. You need to find out all you can about the actual company behind him."

"Yes, and we need to get all the tenants together, put pressure on them."

"Surely the Kapoors have a fair bit left on their lease. I'm sure Ashmara said they renewed it a few years ago."

"Five years, I think she said. But I'll check. Thanks, Mrs. - I mean, Teresa. You're right, there's a few things we can try yet."

"You need an expert in tenants' rights, business tenants in particular."

"I'll get Daniel to ask the solicitor to recommend someone," Denise said. "We can't just lie down and take it. Oh, here's Dan now!"

Dan emerged from the tiny office at the back of the cafe, his face a picture of worry. Slight in build, but wiry, he usually had a cheerful expression and a ready smile. Today, he looked miserable.

"I was telling Mrs. O'Brien about our landlord woes." Denise found it hard to break the habit of calling her by her formal name.

"It's a mess. Pollard - Liam Pollard, that's their rep - he just wouldn't listen."

"And did he address any of the issues you've been having? The damp in the Bald Bear is a disgrace."

"Just shrugged and said he's not interested. But they're the management company, it's their job."

"Hmm. Well, take a note of every issue, flag them in writing too. They have legal obligations and you're still their tenants."

"If I organize a meeting - do you think other businesses would help?" Denise asked. "Like, it'll affect the whole street if three businesses go and our units are left empty!"

"It certainly will, and I'm sure you'll have everyone's support. You're absolutely right, it's in all our interests that the street remains vibrant."

"I contacted the city council too, and there's a group for business owners. A lovely chap there called Fran said he would do all he could to raise awareness. He gave me the names of some councillors to invite."

"Not Seamus Molloy, I take it?"

Denise laughed. "Not on your life. Although I bet he'll try to slither in regardless. Especially if we can get media coverage."

"Let's get started first," Teresa smiled.

She took her leave, happy to see the cafe owners looking a little more hopeful. It was worrying, she thought, but a lot can happen in a year. Maybe there'll be a change of heart. Or this new group might sell on the building, to someone more reasonable. Stranger things had happened. Yes, anything could happen in a year.

Turns out, she didn't have to wait that long for something to happen.

Chapter 2

Barely a week later, Denise had organized the first meeting of the *West Stephen Street Independent Traders Protest Group* or as Michael insisted on calling it, the Anti-Greed League. Denise just laughed at him, and pointed out that her version made a neat acronym - the WE SIT Protest Group. "It'll look good on posters."

"Hopefully it won't come to that," Teresa said.

"Well, even if we're only communicating with the head office of this Southside Development firm, it will look better. We want them to see us as professional and organized."

"Daniel Riordan is lucky to have you," Michael said. "You're a powerhouse once you get stuck into something."

A wistful look passed over her face. "Ah sure, he's that used to me he doesn't hardly know I'm there."

Mrs. O'Brien cast a stern look at Michael, to stop him from making any more blunders. It was an open secret among the business community that Denise was hopelessly attached to her best friend and business partner, but Dan himself seemed oblivious.

"You can count on us," she said quickly, "We'll be there tomorrow night, ready for action."

"Great, thanks!"

When the cafe owner had taken her leave, Teresa looked sharply at her young employee.

"Honestly, Michael, you know she has a huge crush on Dan. You should be careful what you say."

"Me? What did I say?"

She rolled her eyes. "You're as thick, sometimes."

"Am I? Ah sure, she knows I don't mean anything by it. Though it might be as well for the pair of them if she did make her feelings known. They can't go on, him obsessed with selling cakes and her obsessed with him!"

"Really? And how are things with the lovely Lisa?"

Michael had recently fallen for the charms of a young violinist in the Hibernian Symphony Orchestra and was hard at work wooing her. His shy nature and the fact he had placed Lisa on a pedestal of giddy heights ensured he had so far only managed to ask her out for a few dates. He was in no position to talk.

"It's - it's going well," he tried to sound defiant, but his red cheeks gave him away. "I'm planning a really nice romantic dinner soon. Or a picnic. Or maybe a day out in the country. But it's all in hand."

"G'won with yourself. You'd want to move a bit faster than that or some brash conductor or flashy cellist will swoop her up. It might be September but the weather is set to be beautiful from next week - get her out of the city and do something special. A picnic isn't a bad idea at all. I can recommend some great spots in Wicklow." The elderly woman smiled, remembering several very romantic dates with the late Cathal O'Brien. "And when I say "picnic" I don't mean two ham sandwiches and a limp lettuce leaf. I mean fresh cakes, an "afternoon tea" style spread of finger food, strawberries and cream…you could get Denise to help you there."

Michael beat a retreat to his workrooms before Teresa bullied him into texting Lisa there and then. Although he had to admit it was an attractive plan - the next half hour was spent in a happy daydream involving an admiring Lisa and a sumptuous spread of goodies.

Teresa had no time for daydreaming as the shop enjoyed brisk trade that afternoon. Between children needing spare strings before their exams and a steady stream of tourists eager to learn about Irish traditional music, the day passed in a pleasant and productive manner. The following day was just as busy, unusually so for a Friday, and she was quite tired by closing time. Michael eyed her anxiously.

"Are you sure you should come to the meeting? Denise will understand if you're too tired."

Privately he thought, *she's a great woman for seventy but even Teresa O'Brien has her limits.*
"Nonsense. I'm not tired! Besides, all we'll have to do is sit and sip coffee. It's hardly that strenuous."

She made a point of walking briskly down the street to the cafe, feeling quite annoyed at the suggestion that she would cry off on such an important event. She was hardly a decrepit old woman just yet! Distracted by her desire to prove she was full of energy, she pulled the door open and strode in, only then realizing several things at once.

In this order, she realized that they were the first to arrive. There was no Denise behind the counter and while the tables had obviously been rearranged to accommodate the WE SITS meeting, and there were leaflets in neat piles on the counter-top, none of the other shopkeepers were present yet.

Secondly, the place was only lit by a couple of table lamps, decorative ones used to give ambiance rather than illumination. This contributed to her slowness in noticing the third issue.

Dan, her friendly neighbour, was standing over the prone figure of a man. In his hand was a large kitchen knife, with a quantity of something red pooling at his feet. At the sight of Michael and Teresa, his face crumpled and the knife slipped from his hand.

"I- I found him like this!" His voice was a strangled whisper.

"Dan! What happened?" Teresa swung into action, stepping forward and drawing the distraught cafe owner away from the body. "Is he - have you checked for a pulse?"

"What? No - no, I only saw him a few seconds ago."

"Michael, can you?"

Poor Michael, she thought, it was the second time he'd seen a victim of violence up close. The last time he had almost frozen in place, no use to man nor beast for at least half an hour. This time he reacted with a far cooler head, moving quickly to the man on the floor, careful not to disturb him more than was necessary. With his fingers on the man's pulse, he waited anxiously, but it was no use.

"Nothing." He shook his head.

Teresa pushed Dan into the nearest chair. "I'll ring the Gardaí." She pulled out her mobile phone and dialled nine, nine, nine. When prompted she gave the address, asked for the Gardaí and explained that a man had been hurt, badly so. The emergency operator reassured her that an ambulance would be dispatched as well, but it was a moot point. Even before Michael had checked, she had known from the look of him that an ambulance would be too late. However, she went back to the poor dead man and sat on a chair nearby. It seemed indecent to leave him there, uncovered, but she knew better than to disturb a crime scene - a lifetime watching crime dramas and reading mystery novels had its uses. She offered up a silent prayer to whomever and whatever the man had believed in. Michael stood beside her, his head bowed. He wasn't religious in the slightest, but she appreciated his respect. Dan moved closer and sat on the other side of her. They waited in silence.

After what felt like an hour, but her watch showed was only fifteen minutes, sirens broke the spell. Two burly paramedics rushed in, and the three of them retreated to the counter, watching as the medics examined the body. She noticed how careful they were, even as they went through the formalities, obviously aware that they had arrived too late to save him and that the scene had to be preserved.

She realized too that while it wouldn't be long before the Gardaí reached them, it would be only minutes before the Kapoors, Mr. Khan and Paddy Lynch arrived. Plus Maire, from the Irish Design shop, and the staff of WebWide. There would be at least a few more, and they would have to be headed off.

"Michael, go outside and stop anyone coming in. Dan, where is Denise?"

Dan stared at her. "Denise? She's out - she went out to borrow some glasses from Alice." Alice Pierce was the manager of the Millennium, a very popular restaurant attached to the St Stephen hotel at the end of the street.

"Michael," she called, "Denise should be on her way back, let her know what's happening when you see her."

She turned back to Dan. Time was of the essence, she felt. In a very few minutes, it would be in the hands of some detective garda who wouldn't know him, would think the worst of him. "Tell me exactly what happened, quickly."

"I didn't hurt him. I swear it. Denise went to get extra glasses, ours are in the dishwasher. I was putting away the menus in the office when I heard the door opening. Like, I assumed it was someone for the meeting and I called out, *take a seat*, but no one answered. It's hard to be heard from back there, so I came out to see who it was, and there was this person lying on the ground."

"Honestly, I didn't realize what was happening. I thought he'd fallen or fainted or something. Oh - I touched the knife, I wasn't thinking! I saw it lying there and a knife shouldn't be on a dirty floor, so I bent down and picked it up. Then I saw the blood…and that's when you came in."

He looked at her miserably. "It sounds so ridiculous, doesn't it? Who picks a knife up at a crime scene? Will they think I hurt him?"

She looked at him, thinking furiously. "Look, people do stupid things when they're in shock. I'll bet you're not the first person to touch something they shouldn't at a crime scene. You'll be a suspect, but that's only until they start looking into things. Sure, what reason would you have to stab a complete stranger?"

"But he's not. A stranger, I mean. "

"Then who is he? And what is he to you?"

"Mrs. O'Brien - he's the property agent for Southside Developments. He's Liam Pollard - the man who threatened to put me out of business."

"Oh."

It certainly cast a different, and unpleasant, light on the matter. But this was still Dan Riordan. He was a decent person, she would swear to that. It was inconceivable that he would attack someone so viciously, no matter what threat they posed to his business. It was easy perhaps to imagine him punching someone on the nose, in a fair fight, but not stabbing them. She made up her mind.

"Listen to me now. Ask for a solicitor and don't open your mouth until you are assigned one. But then, tell the Gardaí everything, as honestly as possible. Including who he is, how you know him, and why you picked up the knife. Don't be tempted to lie, whatever you do. They'll find out." They both jumped as the door shutter shot up with a metallic whine. "Here's Denise. I'll leave you with her and see what's happening outside."

Michael didn't bother to hide his relief at her reappearance. A few of the locals were milling around talking, obviously curious but reluctant to intrude.

"Everyone is being very good about it. They're mainly worried about Dan." He glanced over her shoulder and remarked, "He looks a bit better now Denise is here."

"She'll mind him. I wish the Gardaí would come, or even the ambulance."

Scanning the small crowd she registered several local faces, including Paddy from the Bald Bear Barbers. Setanta Kapoor was chatting to his granny, Ashmara, and Lily from the Irish Gift Emporium. Beside that group was a well-built man, expensively dressed in a dark blue suit. Councillor Seamus Molloy, she realized. A big name on the city council. There was a stern-looking woman a few feet away, talking to some of the locals. She was also dressed in a dark blue suit, but not an expensive one, and she was slightly flushed. She looked hassled, Teresa thought, or worried. And she kept glancing at Councillor Molloy.

"Look!" Michael pointed to a dark blue sedan car that had

pulled up a few feet away from where they stood. "That looks like an undercover cop car to me."

Sure enough, a uniformed Garda stepped out of the driver's side followed by two burly men in plain clothes. One of them looked to be in his mid-thirties, with a fine head of dark hair and a sharp suit. The other was an older man, with a slightly rumpled air.

"Ah." Teresa poked Michael in the arm. "We know him."

The older detective was Malachy Flynn - and not six months earlier Mrs. O'Brien had helped him solve the murder of a famous violinist.

Chapter 3

Detective Malachy Flynn smiled at Mrs. O'Brien. "I won't say I'm pleased to see you again, not in these circumstances, but it's definitely a consolation."

He was a solid man, who looked to be in his mid fifties, with a broad, pleasant face. His companion hovered at his elbow, obviously anxious to get started. Detective Flynn ignored his impatience, gesturing towards the shuttered entrance to *Fancies.*

"Is it too much to hope that you know what's going on here?" he asked Teresa.

The younger detective looked at him in surprise and gave a little grunt of protest, which just made Detective Flynn's smile even broader.

"Calm yourself, Dempsey. This lady has been a great help to me in a previous case. She's nearly one of us - aren't you, Mrs. O'Brien?"

"Teresa, please. And no, of course not. I was able to help you a little with that awful case, but it's hardly the same thing as being a trained detective."

Her tone was a shade reproving; Detective Flynn was showing a levity hardly becoming to such a serious situation. She smiled at Detective Dempsey.

"I'm please to meet you, Detective."

Dempsey looked a little mollified, and even returned her smile with a cautious twitch of his lips. A lifetime behind a counter observing human nature had given Teresa an excellent insight into people. A young and ambitious detective anxious to impress was very little different from a self-conscious teenager - both just needed a little respect.

"She's being modest," Detective Flynn had a twinkle in his eye. "Well, is there anything we should know before we go in?"

Teresa hesitated, trying to formulate the words. "Someone has been hurt…killed. In my friends' cafe."

She started again, this time ordering her thoughts into a coherent summary. "*Fancies* is run by Denise and Daniel, they're friends not a couple - they usually close at six but we're having a meeting of our business association here. That's why all these people are outside - they're the local shop owners and of course, you'll recognize Councillor Molloy over there. Michael and I arrived slightly early for the meeting. Denise was out, getting extra bits and pieces. Daniel was inside. The door was unlocked so we entered and saw a man lying on the ground. He was dead. You'd better hear the rest from Dan."

The senior Detective nodded appreciatively. "Nicely done, Mrs. O'Brien. I knew I could rely on you. Any idea who the victim is?"

"As I said, you need to speak to Dan. He can explain all that better than I can." She resisted the impulse to describe how Dan had touched the knife. It would be better coming from him. Detective Flynn was a fair man and would appreciate it.

"Well, let's get to it. I'll have a uniformed Garda take your statements, if you and Michael will wait. They can take them in your shop, save you standing out here."

21

With that, he motioned to a young Garda to lift the shutter and open the door. The two detectives entered *Fancies* and Mrs. O'Brien sighed sadly. Daniel was in for a very tough time, even if the Gardaí believed his version of events. The death of a man he had every reason to dislike, on his premises, with no witnesses to back up his story - a very unpleasant position to be in.

Michael took her arm and gave her a little hug.

"Come on, Teresa. Let's go back to ours, and at least sit down while we're waiting. I'll make you a nice cup of tea."

Mr. Khan, from the noodle bar, appeared at her other side. A short, plump man in his forties, with a tonsure of brown hair around a bald pate, he usually greeted everyone with a wide smile. At that moment however, he was grave and serious.

"Mrs. O'Brien, is it true? They say you found a body, in *Fancies.* Are you okay?"

"I'm fine thank you, Mr. Khan. But yes, sadly. A man died tonight."

"That is awful. Poor Dan, and poor Denise. And obviously, poor man too. I am so sorry to hear this. It must have been a shock, for you both."

"It was," Michael interjected. "I'm taking Teresa back to our shop, to rest and we'll give out statements to the Gardaí there."

"Very wise. I will send over some noodles for you, my daughter will bring them over. No, I insist!"

Before they could object, he crossed the street and entered his noodle restaurant. As they let themselves back into the old music shop, they could hear him calling out, "No sauce, just duck! Mai, fresh veg for Mrs. O'Brien!"

"Actually, now he's offered I am a bit hungry," she admitted, sinking gratefully into her office chair.

"I know, it seems callous to think about eating with that poor sod lying dead in there - and Dan in the firing line. But I'm exhausted, and a bite of food will make the next few hours a lot easier." Michael spied a figure at the door. "There's Mai! I'll let her in."

Mai Khan bustled in, her arms full of white paper bags emblazoned with the logo "Khan Noodle Palace" with its distinctive red and black wok and crossed chopsticks.

"Mrs. O'Brien! I can't believe it, Dad just told me. Thank heavens it wasn't someone we knew, but still! You wouldn't be right after that, would you?"

She cleared a space on the computer desk and began to decant the contents of the bags. "Duck noodles, your favourite, no hot sauce. Michael, veg noodles with sweet chili sauce. Two teas - Mam made them, so they'll be drinkable. Dad can never get the hang of a proper cup of tea, not that he'll believe me."

She opened the last bag and carefully lifted out two bundles wrapped in napkins. Michael's eyes lit up as the teenager showed them two slices of strawberry cream gateaux.

"I didn't know ye sold cakes!"

"Sure, we don't. Authentic Asian cuisine all the way. But we'd a birthday party in at lunch and there was a nice bit of cake left over. The birthday girl said we should keep it. A bit of sugar to get over the shock." She brushed her long hair back from her face and perched on the side of the desk. "Now, spill. Who got killed? Did Dan do it?"

"Mai!"

"Ah Mrs. O'Brien, I'm only asking." It was impossible to be annoyed at the sixteen-year-old. She was a bundle of energy and fun, and despite her irreverent manner she was as nice a kid as Teresa had ever met. "Gwon, tell me."

23

"Well…you know we were all meeting up to discuss this new landlord company, the one that bought the building opposite yours? Well, the man who died was the landlord's representative, a sort of estate agent if I understand it correctly."

"Oh! The one Dan talked to, that was so nasty to him?"

"Yes."

"I met him. Liam Pollard. He called into the Palace the day before Dan went to meet him. He was pumping Mam, trying to find out about all the shops in that block. Mam saw through him, the moment he opened his mouth, so she said nothing. But he was absolutely brazen. Asked if the Bald Bear was busy, did Paddy only take cash, and did we know if the Kapoors had more than one business in the shop? Very rude, very nosey."

"That's interesting," Teresa said. "Did you hear anything else?"

"Not really, although - his phone rang, and he went outside to take the call. I was doing my homework at the table near the door and couldn't help overhearing." From her grin, Teresa deduced that she had in fact shamelessly eavesdropped. "He was talking to someone, giving out yards that he didn't appreciate being kept out of the loop. Then he said they'd talk about it later. Whoever he was talking to didn't seem to like that, because he said "I don't care! Either you explain yourself or I'm pulling out.""

"I wonder who he was talking to?" Michael sighed. "Not that it helps, probably. From the sound of it he was difficult with everyone."

"Not a nice man." Mai hopped up. "I'd better go back, Mam will be going batty. Dad's out chatting to everyone, he's so nosey."

Michael laughed as the girl bounced out of the shop. "Pot

calling the kettle names! That kid is as nosey as her dad."

"She's observant, though. Hopefully she'll keep an ear out for any gossip. You never know what might help."

"Help?" Michael eyed her suspiciously. "Was Detective Flynn right? Are you planning on "helping" him?"

"Don't be cheeky. I'm just saying we owe it to Dan to make sure the Gardaí are aware of any information that might help."

He said nothing but his expression spoke volumes. Luckily, distraction arrived in the form of a young Garda at the shop door, ready to take their statements. She was a keen and cheerful young woman, who introduced herself as Garda Jo Maguire - "Jo, short for Josephine" - and proceeded to winkle every detail out of them. She reminded Teresa of a friendly terrier, very pleasant but intent on pursuing every whiff of a trail. It was a tiring end to a very long day, and she was relieved when at last they could lock up and go home.

Michael had an apartment in the area, a small but bright box of glass and concrete above one of the buildings on the main street. Mrs. O'Brien had a short journey home, out to the suburbs, in her little red car. It was old but solid, and still capable of a fine turn of speed when necessary. She was happy to see the inside of her own comfortable house, to sit for a while in her living room with a cup of tea and then up the stairs to bed.

A good night's sleep restored her spirits somewhat. The day was bright and sunny, warm enough that she could take her breakfast out onto the deck in her back garden and enjoy the birdsong. Her late husband had built the decking, and in his typical fashion had made it solid, functional and very slightly wonky. She smiled every time she saw the mismatched posts on the little steps leading to the grass. "Cathal, you never got around to fixing them!" she would point out, and she could almost hear his voice replying, "Ah sure, time enough."

"We ran out of time though, pet," She thought. "But the deck is still standing, like myself."

Spending time in her garden always cheered her up. By the time she was ready to leave for work, she was reasonably hopeful that the Gardaí would already have ruled Dan out as a credible suspect. After all, if everyone with a reason to dislike landlords went around bumping them or their representatives off, Dublin would have a lot fewer landlords and less of a housing crisis.

Saturdays were always the busiest day of the week especially now that tourists had begun to flock back to the city. When she opened up, there was no sign of anyone in Fancies but that was hardly surprising. She couldn't imagine Denise selling honey cakes and making small talk with the place barely cleared of forensic officers. She had spotted the famous Dr. Lorraine O'Toole in the crowd of white boiler suits busying themselves around the cafe the night before. The state pathologist was known for her thoroughness and it could be days before the cafe would be allowed to reopen.

Assuming you'd want to reopen, with the memory of a dead body haunting you.

There wasn't much time for worrying about it. The morning was filled with two families requiring new violins, a group of cheerful Americans looking for tin whistles, bodhráns and a bit of local history and Finbar O'Leary, who was so pleased with his newly repaired mandolin, he gave an impromptu concert in the shop to the delight of the tourists.

Before he left, the mandolin player pulled her aside.

"I saw the news last night - terrible business next door."

"It certainly was!" She agreed.

"Well, just between us - I recognized the man. Pollard. He worked with my brother, years ago. A difficult man, very difficult. But he was straight enough, for an estate agent."

She didn't comment - people can change a lot over the course of decades. It felt churlish to contradict Finbar and say what a horrible person Pollard had turned out to be. Especially when the unfortunate man was dead.

At lunchtime, Teresa wandered out to see if there was any news. Neither the Kapoors nor the Khans had heard anything fresh, but Paddy Lynch called her in to the Bald Bear Barbers. He was elbow deep in a head of long curly hair, the owner of which had a face she vaguely recognized. A singer or guitar player...on the telly, recently...it clicked suddenly. BoBo, the lead singer of The Blackberries, often called the most famous Irish rock band in history. He was no Phil Lynott in her opinion but he was a consummate showman, famous for tossing his long locks and head banging around the stage, as the crowd roared in approval. It was quite impressive that he chose her neighbour as his barber.

Paddy winked at her over BoBo's head and mouthed, "I'll only be a minute!" A girl appeared at her side, guided her to a large armchair and fetched a coffee with custard cream biscuits.

"Pad will be with you shortly," she murmured. Teresa smiled and sipped the excellent coffee as she took in the clientele of the salon. Beautiful young people, she thought, all so fashionable and well groomed. There was a girl getting one side of her hair shaved, and the other side a few inches in length, was being dyed a bright purple. In the chair beside her a young man with a beard that would have been impressive in Dickens' day was receiving what looked like a head massage. You could hardly tell the hairdressers from the clients, all of them so young and dressed in the coolest, newest fashions. The eldest by far was Paddy, but he dressed as well as any of them - today sporting a multicoloured shirt, reminiscent of a peacock, with the sleeves rolled up to show off well-defined arm muscles and his dark hair coiffed into a wave across the top of his head, the ends dyed magenta.

As she admired his outfit, he stepped back from the rock star and nodded. "Perfect."

BoBo examined himself anxiously in the mirror, while Paddy held up a mirror behind him so he could see the back of his head.

"Man, you're a genius!"

"I know." Paddy smiled and put his hands on BoBo's shoulders.

"You will look like a *god* on stage," he announced solemnly. "This is my best yet."

The singer jumped to his feet and shook Paddy's hand.

"You don't know what that means to me, man. Thank you. I'll see you soon."

Paddy escorted BoBo to the door, then threw himself into the armchair beside Mrs. O'Brien.

"Oh my gawd. He's an awful nice fella but so self conscious. He pops in every time he's got a tour coming up. Like, all I do is a blow-dry and a bit of mousse but he's convinced no one else can do it. I used to do his hair when The Blackberries were starting off. They're all a bit superstitious about it."

He leaned forward conspiratorially. "I was the one that told him to head-bang on stage. It's his signature move. "Show off that head of hair," I told him and he did, the very night a record label scout was in the audience. They were playing in the old

Baggot Inn - he started throwing his hair around, the crowd went wild, the rest is history."

He leaned back and grinned. "They all still come to me, when they're in Ireland. It's half the reason we're packed every day. People are only dying to tell their friends they were getting a blow dry next to BoBo."

Teresa laughed. "Well, it's nice they're loyal to you."

"Ah lovely bunch of lads. But never mind all that, have you heard anything from Denise, or poor Dan?"

"No, not since last night. I texted them both, but no reply yet. Have you?"

"No, but…actually, I'm really glad you called in. I was hoping to talk to you. You know the victim was Liam Pollard, he's handling things for the new landlords?"

"Yes, Dan told me."

"Well, I haven't said it to the Gardaí yet, but Pollard was around here several times last week."

"Mai said he was in their place the day before he met Dan. He was very nosey, apparently."

Paddy nodded. "He was in here, asking about our rental situation. Pretended to be a business owner, looking for a similar unit. Asked if we were thinking of moving or if any of the businesses were doing badly…I soon copped on though. He wasn't as clever as he thought."

"That's interesting," Teresa frowned. "Surely as the landlord's rep he would have had access to all that information anyway. Why come around here showing his hand?"

"I don't know," Paddy shrugged. "But anyway, I told Dan about it. He was…well, he was furious. Like, he said that Pollard had led him on a merry dance, pretending to be open to a discussion, but was obviously intent on getting us all out.

I wasn't impressed myself, but he was really upset."

Paddy's bright green eyes met Mrs. O'Brien's soft hazel ones and he said quietly, "He did say he'd like to punch him. Obviously not something I'd say to anyone else- but, between us, is it possible he lost his head and did something in a temper?"

"I - I honestly don't know, Paddy. But I find it hard to imagine. I've seen Dan deal with really horrible customers, and while he has a temper, he is far more likely to throw something at the wall than actually hurt a person."

"I do agree, but you just don't know - do you? I wouldn't blame him either. Like, I'm fairly sure my lease is unbreakable, and I don't think they can raise my rent outside the agreed terms, but the lease on *Fancies* is up next year. If they don't negotiate decent terms, poor Dan is out. It's all they have, him and Denise."

Thanking Paddy for the coffee and chat, Mrs. O'Brien made her way slowly back to the music shop. She mulled over what Paddy had told her. It was true, no one knew what would push a person over the edge. Was it possible that Daniel had stabbed Liam Pollard in a fit of temper?

The same kind Dan who was so friendly and helpful?

Her mobile phone made a loud pinging noise. A new text - her heart beat a little faster as she saw "Denise Burke" flash up on the screen. The text was short and made Teresa inhale sharply.

"Please help. Daniel was arrested for murder."

Chapter 4

"It's all a horrible mistake!" Denise wailed, her face half buried in a damp tissue. She had arrived at *Fancies*, tearful and shaking, to find both Teresa and Michael waiting for her.

"And you two should be back at work, you can't be shutting on a Saturday!"

"For goodness' sake, Denise," Teresa's tone was brisk. "We shut up shop a bit early. No one will mind. Now, I understand you're upset but this is not helping anyone. Least of all, Daniel."

Denise sniffed. "But I don't know what to do -"

"Neither do I," Teresa cut her off before she could recap on the horrors of having her innocent partner arrested for murder. "But if we put our heads together, we might be able to come up with something."

She nodded in approval as the younger woman took a deep breath, wiped her eyes and straightened up.

"You're right," Denise said firmly. "There's no point in crying over it all. Dan needs us."

"That's the spirit," Michael placed a fresh coffee in front of her and emptied a pack of brown sugar into it. "For the shock. Have you eaten? I found some pastries in your fridge, might as well use them up."

Denise managed a wobbly smile. "You're right. I haven't eaten since yesterday. I was too nervous before the meeting, and then -"

"Sure, you'll feel better after eating."

Michael had grown up with a mother, a typical Irish Mammy, who believed food cured all ills. Cold? Feed it with hot soup and bread. Heartbreak? Serve up some cakes and sweets. Broken leg? Well, okay -you'd probably need a doctor first but *then*, a nice plate of ham sandwiches and a pot of strong tea.

Mrs Clancy's theory of medicinal food certainly worked its magic on Denise. With every sip of coffee and bite of pastry, some colour returned to her cheeks.

"I didn't realize how hungry I was until I started eating!" she confessed, adding "I'm sorry about earlier."

"Don't be silly. You have every right to be upset. But now it's time to concentrate on helping Dan."

"You're right, Teresa, of course, but I can't think what to do. He has a solicitor. His brother has an old school friend who was happy to step in. I can't visit him until they let me, his brother got in for a few minutes this morning but that's it for now. If they charge him..." She swallowed a sob and continued, "Well, we'll be visiting him in remand then. Unless he gets bail, of course. I don't even know how any of that works."

"Leave that to his brother," Teresa advised. "Dan needs your support, whatever happens. In the meantime, we have a few avenues we can explore."

Both Denise and Michael stared at her. Denise looked hopeful while Michael looked apprehensive. Mrs. O'Brien ignored both of them and continued.

"We know Liam Pollard was sniffing around for days before

his meeting with Dan. We could try to find out why. Also, why did he come to *Fancies* that evening? To spy on the meeting? To try and stop us organizing? Or to put the landlord's point of view to the group?"

"That's for the police to find out," Michael's tone was firm.

"Never said it wasn't." Teresa had a stubborn streak, when pushed. "But it won't do any harm to ask around a bit, see what we can find out. I've already spoken to Paddy Lynch. Mai told us about Pollard's visit to the Noodle Palace. We do a little digging, and if we find out anything interesting - we'll pass it on to Detective Flynn."

"Hmm." Michael was unconvinced.

Denise was delighted.

"Mrs. O'Brien! You're a genius. Let's do it. It's better than sitting around waiting to hear the worst. But where do we start?"

Teresa considered carefully. "It seems to me the most important thing is to find out a bit more about Liam Pollard. So far, we know he was employed by Southside Developments. He seems to have been some class of an estate agent, representing their interests. We know he was rude, unreasonable and unpleasant, but that is neither here nor there. I think I should try to find out more about his business - do you know what it's called?"

"Eh…yes, hang on." Denise fished a card out of her wallet. "Here it is, Liam Pollard and the firm is *Brook and Pollard Ltd, Commercial Property Experts.*""

Teresa took the card and entered the number in her phone. "Brook must be his partner. I bet if I ring up and say I've a building on this street that I'd like to rent out…"

"Oh!" Denise clapped her hands. "Sneaky. I like it!"

"I bet he'll jump at the chance to value the building, especially with commercial rents so high at the moment. Once I get a chance to talk to him, maybe we can find out more about Pollard."

"You're not going to meet this Brook character, not on your own." Michael frowned. "If he wants to have a face to face, tell him to come to the shop. I'll be there, just in case."

Teresa nodded. "No harm in being careful. Now, Denise - your job is to find out everything you can about Southside Developments. Reach out to all the other tenants, find out if anyone knows who owns it or anything at all about it. Try online too. Your accountants might be able to help…ask them how we can find out company information and so on."

Gone was the weeping woman of only half an hour ago, and in her place was capable and proactive Denise. "Will do."

"Now, the Gardaí will trace Pollard's movements yesterday evening. They can check CCTV footage and the like. But we know he's been around all last week, asking people questions. Michael, you talk to everyone on the street, find out what he was up to."

For a moment Michael looked as if he was about to protest but like the good young man he was, he bowed to the inevitable and said, "Yes, Mrs. O'Brien."

"And what's my job?" The three conspirators jumped in fright and turned in unison, only to find Mai Khan standing behind them, her arms crossed and a cheeky grin on her face.

"What…what are you doing here, Mai?" Denise asked weakly.

"I saw the shutters up and came in to make sure you were okay," the teenager said. "I couldn't help overhearing you. I totally agree with Mrs. O'Brien, we should try to help clear Dan's name."

"This is a serious issue, Mai," Teresa said. "I'm sure your heart is in the right place but you must understand - it's not a game."

"I'm sixteen, not six - with all due respect. Look, I know more about what goes on around here than any of you. Everyone talks in front of me like I'm part of the furniture. I'm in and out of every shop in the area in my spare time, delivering food. My mother is the biggest gossip in the whole of Dublin and my dad is a close runner. It's the family superpower. You have to let me help."

The adults tried not to smile. Mai pressed home her advantage.

"I was the one who told you about Pollard being around last week. And I know where's he been, which shops he was sniffing around. I know - for example - that he was *very* interested in the music shop. Aha! See - you didn't know that, did you. " She threw herself onto one of the cafe's deep leather couches. "You need me. Any of those pastries left?"

Teresa gave up. There seemed little point in resisting and it was probably better to have Mai under their eyes than running around on her own.

"Here, there's one almond slice left and a bit of carrot cake. Now, what's this about the music shop?"

"Pollard was in the stationery shop around the corner, the Pen and Paper. Lovely stuff in there, all kinds of journals. I'm going to start a journal, record my life. Maybe a leather bound one. Anyway…he asked them and other people if they knew you, if you owned the building, were you not thinking of retiring soon. "A*t her advanced age,*" I believe was the exact phrase."

Teresa snorted.

"*We* don't think you're past it," Mai reassured her, "but you can see how it might look to someone who didn't realize you're as tough as old boots. Anyway, Maggie that runs the place gave him short shrift. Told him he'd be better off asking you directly and not creeping around behind your back. She's very direct, is Maggie. Between you and me, I'm not entirely sure she's suited to retail."

Michael smothered a laugh. "She is a bit brusque at times."

"Pollard also asked about the shops around on the main road," Mai took a bite of cake and added smugly, "I think this Southside lot want to buy up the whole corner block."

"There was talk of that a few years ago," Teresa mused. "Wanted to build a shopping centre. But no one was interested in selling. And they couldn't have proceeded anyway. My building is a Grade Two Listed building, they can't just knock it down."

"You know, I wouldn't bet on it," Michael said. "I believe there are a few projects where all they had to do was keep the facade of the old building, but they ripped the rest apart."

Teresa shuddered. "Not if I can help it." She thought of the three story, old brick building with its two centuries of history. "Really, I'm not against progress but they shouldn't be allowed to destroy everything that makes Dublin unique!"

"Ring Brook," Mai advised. "Pretend you're old and doddery and ready to sell up. See if he bites."

"And when we have him interested, pump him for every bit of information we can. Sounds like a plan to me."

Chapter 5

Mr Eugene Brook sniffed appreciatively and remarked, "Three stories, no less. And a cellar? It's very old fashioned of course, but a small investment in modernization would bring the building up to spec - could add twenty percent or more to your yearly rental. I'd advise splitting it up into units…three separate tenants paying a healthy monthly rate is better than relying on one client."

He paused and nodded. "Yes, I think we could get you quite a good return on any outlay. When do you see yourself retiring?"

Teresa tried not to take offense. After all, she had rung and invited the man to give the old building the once over - on the very pretext that she was looking to retire. Now that he was here in front of her, nosing into everything and making disparaging comments about the place, it was harder than she had expected.

"I'm a silly old woman," she thought, "I just don't like thinking about retiring, even in jest." She tried to look both impressed and interested, not that Brook needed much encouragement to talk. The man had barely drawn breath since entering the shop.

She let his prattle wash over her while she took stock of the estate agent - or Commercial Property Expert, as he insisted on being called. He looked to be around the same age as Liam Pollard; early forties, at a guess. Tall, skinny, with sandy-coloured hair already thinning, and a pinched face, he peered out from behind round, rimless glasses. He reminded her of an inquisitive weasel.

"I'm not entirely sure when I will retire, Mr. Brook."

"Hmm. Well, it's up to you of course - but if you'll take my advice, you should take advantage of the current market. The demand for premises in this area is very high. And once you have tenants locked in to a lease, we can manage it for you. Of course, if it were me -" He gave her a sharp glance, "I'd sell up entirely. Then you'd have a lump sum and no worries. You'll be able to relax and enjoy your twilight years."

Twilight years! Teresa could hear a stifled giggle from the office. Michael and Mai were both there, listening. The original plan had not included Mai, whom she assumed would be at school on a Monday afternoon, in nearby St Etna's on St Stephen's Green, but she had underestimated the teenager. She had turned up, triumphantly proclaimed "Free period," and made herself at home in the back of the shop.

"I can study here as easily as in school," Mai had grinned.

As she had also thoughtfully brought cakes from the local bakers, neither Teresa nor Michael had protested strongly. Teresa regretted this slightly now, listening to the giggling behind her. She turned her attention back to Eugene Brook.

"Indeed. Well, thank you for your advice. I will certainly bear it in mind. Might I ask, do you have a lot of experience in this area?"

"In Commercial Property?" Brook looked outraged. "I can say with confidence, there are few firms in the city with more experience than mine!"

"Oh yes, I gathered that. I meant more, this area…literally. This part of the city. I know you are dealing with a nearby building, one of my neighbours told me. But that's very recent, I understand?"

"Ah. My apologies, I didn't quite catch your drift. Yes, we have handled quite a few properties in this area." He waved his hand loftily. "And we actually handle the building next door to you, perhaps that's what your neighbour meant? We are representatives of Southside Developments, who acquired the building a few months ago."

"Ah yes, that was it. I remember now. Oh! I've just realized - you must have known that poor man who was killed?"

Mr. Brook looked somber. "Ah. Yes, indeed. Liam Pollard was my partner."

"Brook and Pollard? I'm so sorry, I never realized. You must think I'm very slow."

"Not at all," he replied politely.

"It's such a difficult time for you," she rattled on, "And you must find it so hard to carry on! Such a tragedy."

"Yes, he will be greatly missed. Now, about these renovations…"

"So young, too. It's a disgrace. I remember when this city was safe - now it's all robberies, stabbings, young people running amuck!"

The estate agent tilted his head. "Ah. I couldn't agree more. It's all gone downhill in recent years, hasn't it? It can't be easy for a lady of your years, it's not very safe to be in retail these days."

Another stifled laugh from the office - this time it was Michael. Teresa bit down on the urge to put Mr Commercial

39

Property Expert in his place and instead looked suitably mournful. "Oh, it's terrible. I never thought I'd consider retirement so early, but - well, the area isn't what it used to be."

"Ah. The whole city has changed, I'm afraid. You have quite an eclectic mix of neighbours, don't you? I mean, Irish handmade goods on one side, and then that... "Asian Cuisine," shall we say? And the huckster shop selling outlandish clothes on the other side. Can't do much for business, can it?"

There was no more laughter from the pair in the office. Mrs. O'Brien could only hope neither Mai nor Michael would charge out and give the horrible man a thump. She tried to keep her face composed, and her voice pleasant. "It's not that I've anything against them -" She let the rest of sentence unspoken, hanging between them. He winked in response.

"I quite understand, Mrs. O'Brien. Ah, it's very difficult these days. But there's more than one way to skin a cat, I always say. There'll be a clean sweep soon enough, get rid of all the piddling little shops and get in some real businesses. There are plenty of sensible men in politics these days, believe me. They're just as anxious as you or me that the city remains...*respectable*. Councillor Molloy has a particular interest in this area, and he's a man of vision. Take next door for example. The whole bottom floor of that building could make one decent retail outlet - plenty of international brands looking to set up in Dublin's centre. And if you did want to sell, you'd find them very generous in my experience..."

She had to admire how adroitly he worked his sales pitch into every conversation. It was about the only thing to admire about him.

"That's really interesting, Mr. Brook. I have a lot to think about. I do appreciate your help! Especially at such a difficult time. Poor Mr. Pollard, I suppose he was at that silly meeting to talk sense into your tenants?"

Brook blinked rapidly. "I suppose so. I mean, yes. He didn't tell me he was going but it makes sense. He was probably lured there by that mad café owner."

"How awful. And to think, he'll never see your great plans for the place come to fruition. I do hope you won't allow them to derail you?"

"Not a chance. They can protest all they want, but one by one we'll get them out."

"We? Is there another partner? I thought it was just Brook and Pollard?"

He glanced at her sharply and she smiled vaguely, her "I'm just a little old woman" smile. No one who knew her would have been fooled but it seemed to reassure the man.

"Ah, no. Just myself, now. By we, I mean the property owners obviously."

"Ah, silly of me."

It took a while to shift Brook from the shop. Even as she escorted him to the door, he continued to press her to commit to selling or at least renting out the building and only the appearance of customers persuaded him to go. Teresa heaved a sigh of relief and gave a heartfelt welcome to the musicians, ukulele players from a well-known Dublin group called the Super Ukers. Ukulele was a very popular instrument in Ireland and its aficionados were among her favourite customers. Cheerful, friendly people who loved music and performing, the ukulele players found a home in the old music shop. Cathal, bless his departed soul, was a great man for violins and cellos, regarding the humble ukulele with suspicion. But Teresa O'Brien fell in love with them, knew every type and make, and loved nothing more than discussing the relative merits of solid mahogany versus aged cedar.

"Mrs. O'Brien!" Clara, a lady in her fifties with bright red hair and an air of glamour, greeted her. "We nearly died when we saw the news the other day. Stabbing on West Stephen Street…I shouted at Peadair, didn't I?"

Her husband nodded solemnly. He was a quiet man by nature, which was just as well.

"I shouted, "Peadair, it's poor Mrs. O'Brien, she's been stabbed!" but it wasn't you at all, which was brilliant news."

Catherine, a tall and willowy girl with long blonde hair, smiled gently. "Clara means, we're all just happy you are okay."

"I am okay, and I know what Clara meant," she replied. "It was a shock to us too." "Were you there?" Eamonn, a giant of a young man and one of her particular favourites, looked at her anxiously. Teresa hesitated but decided to be frank. "Yes, Michael and I found the body. Clara, that's not common knowledge, so don't say that to anyone."

"I won't, honest. I know I talk a lot but I can keep a secret when I have to. Finding the body - that must have been rotten." Clara paused then added, "You found that body in the Concert Hall, too. It's getting to be a habit, isn't it?"

"Clara!" The other three ukulele players exclaimed in unison. Teresa sighed. She was very fond of the woman but by the holy Bridgets, she had no filter.

"It's not a habit I want to get into, Clara. But it happened, and now we've to deal with it."

"Peadair doesn't think that fella from next door did it, do you, Peadair? He went on and on about it last night, how he wasn't that type - didn't you, Peadair?"

Peadair nodded.

42

"Peadair thinks he's been set up. Like in that drama on TV - the one with the man who was in the film about the cat. He adopted it in the end. The cat, I mean. In the TV series though, he was framed for murder. Peadair thinks your neighbour is being framed."

Everyone took a moment to work through the confused statement. Eamonn got there first. "Yes, I agree. I've had coffee there loads of times. Dan is really nice, I can't see him murdering anyone."

Catherine wandered down to the largest showcase and picked up her current favourite ukulele.

"Hello, beauty," she said, strumming the Kala Macawood Tenor and humming. She looked pensive, and Teresa eyed her curiously. You would never think it to look at her, but the girl had a mind like a steel trap, underneath the dreamy air.

Mai appeared from the office, her schoolbag over one shoulder. "I need to go back to school." She was unusually subdued.

"Mai, that man is a pig," Teresa said. "I would have given him a piece of my mind under normal circumstances, but -"

"It's okay, Mrs. O'Brien, I know that. It's just - you get a bit sick of hearing things like that. I was born here. My parents have been here for yonks. My granny is buried here! But he thinks we're just blow-ins."

Eamonn scowled. "What's this?"

Teresa glanced at Mai. "I had a visitor, that man you saw leaving. He's an estate agent. He made some - rude remarks."

"About Mai's family? And why didn't you tell him to shove off?"

"It's not her fault!" Mai turned on the big lad. "We were investigating. She couldn't blow her cover."

43

The others stared at her and then at Teresa. The silence lasted quite a long time.

"Okay." Peadair finally spoke. "I think you'd better elaborate on *"investigating"* and how she was *"under cover.""*

Teresa sighed. "I can see we're going to have to explain."

Chapter 6

The ukulele players listened attentively as Mrs. O'Brien, Michael and Mai filled them in on everything that had happened. Catherine in particular was interested in the whole property aspect - and to Teresa's surprise, revealed herself to be a solicitor specializing in commercial property.

"I know of Brook and Pollard," Catherine remarked. "My firm has dealt with them a few times - from the other side. Not me, personally, but colleagues have represented tenants and even other property firms occasionally. Brook and Pollard have a reputation for being ruthless, and although I wouldn't say this officially, a lot of people think they're downright unscrupulous."

"Pollard seems to have been a right pain," Teresa remarked. "Shouldn't speak ill of the dead and all that, but - he was pig ignorant to Dan and Denise about their lease."

"I agree," Michael said, "but for all that, it's Brook I would have called the least trustworthy. From the sound of it, Pollard was brusque and inflexible but Brook makes my skin crawl."

Mai giggled. "He certainly managed to insult me, and Mrs. O'Brien."

Teresa sniffed. "Well, it's not as bad as his nasty little comments about my neighbours -I'm so sorry you had to hear that, Mai - but I didn't appreciate him speaking to me like I'd one foot in the grave. I'm not that old!"

Everyone else avoided making eye contact.

"Mrs. O'Brien, what *do* you think happened?" Clara tilted her head to one side, like an inquisitive bird. "Pollard must have been attending the meeting for the business owners for some reason."

"There are a few possibilities. He might have turned up to spy, or to intimidate - maybe hoped to bully Dan before the meeting started. Or he was there to meet someone."

"Someone lured him there, you mean?" Mai interjected.

"Well - that's certainly possible. That's an interesting idea, Mai. Of course, he may simply know some of the attendees and wanted to talk to them."

Teresa thought for a moment.

"Detective Flynn may well know why he attended. I think I might have a chance of getting the information from him. At any rate, it's worth a try."

"You need to consider who wanted him dead, besides Dan," Eamonn said. "Maybe one of the other tenants had even more reason to hate him?"

Mai produced a notebook from her schoolbag and scribbled furiously. "This is good stuff, keep it coming."

"Don't you have school?" Teresa asked pointedly.

"*Double* free period." Mai grinned. "I'll be back in plenty of time. Now, we've got "Was Pollard lured to meeting?" and "Who hated him more than Dan?" What else?"

"Well, what about Pollard's personal life? Maybe this has nothing to do with the building. Like, has he left behind a load of money and a merry widow?" Clara waved her hands expressively. "Maybe we should be looking at that!"

Mai nodded, adding it to her list.

"I dunno, Clara," Eamonn, like Catherine, had taken up a ukulele and was strumming it. He paused and gazed thoughtfully into space. "What about this mysterious new property company, Southside? They take over and all hell breaks lose. I'd start there."

"Good, you do that." Mai pointed at each of them in turn. "Clara, you take his personal life. Mrs. O'Brien will pump the good Detective for information, and Michael and I will see who had meetings with Pollard, and who else was threatened with immediate eviction."

Catherine played a few bars of Fulsome Blues. "I'll find out everything I can about Brook, and his role in all this."

Peadair nodded. "I have a few contacts in commercial property. I'll take Brook and see what I can find out about the man."

"Wait a minute!" Teresa looked at the group in alarm. "Look, we only started poking around to help Denise, give her something to do. This is getting out of hand. I never intended for all of you to get involved…"

"Ah whist." Clara spoke for the ukulele players. "We're getting ourselves involved. Can't have these bully boy developers ruining our city! I'll chain myself to railings before I'd let them turn this street into another generic shopping centre."

"Hear, hear!" Eamonn cheered. "If poking around helps Dan even a little bit and stops them rolling over the little shops, I'm in."

"After rehearsals!" Catherine squealed, pointing to her watch. "We're dead late."

"Mark will kill us," Eamonn moaned, reluctantly handing a mahogany soprano back to Teresa. "I love this one, Mrs.

O'Brien. Any chance you could put it aside for me, until I get paid? End of the week, no later."

"Of course I will, Eamonn. Gwon now, and don't you lot be worrying about Dan. There's no need for you to get involved." Her words fell on deaf ears, the four ignoring her and instead winking at Mai and Michael as they went.

"Surely you agree, Michael," Teresa pleaded. "We shouldn't get them involved."

"Safety in numbers, Mrs. O'Brien," Michael shrugged. "I'd sooner they poked around than you, frankly."

Tutting and muttering under her breath, Teresa busied herself with her precious instruments, hanging the ukes back up and rearranging some of them to better catch the eye. Mai grinned at her and made a thumbs up gesture to Michael, her eyes twinkling.

"I'm off now, Mrs. O'Brien. Let me know how you get on with Detective Flynn. Oh, and let us know if you hear from Denise - maybe she's got in to see Dan by now!"

Teresa waved goodbye to the teenager, but pointedly ignored Michael. Really, what was it will all these young whippersnappers telling her she was past it?

The day wore on, uninterrupted by any further talk of murder. She was home and sipping tea when her phone rang, Detective Flynn's number popping up on the screen.

"Mrs. O'Brien? Malachy Flynn here. I hope I'm not disturbing you?"

"Not at all."

"Ah, good. Good. I wanted to make sure you're doing all right, that was a bad shock."

"I'm grand, thanks. Well, not grand exactly - but not too bad. Of course, it was also a shock to hear that poor Dan was arrested." She let the reproach hang in the air.

"Ah. Yes. Quite." He heaved a sigh. "I'm not too happy about it myself, if I'm honest."

She perked up. "You're not?"

"Just between ourselves, you understand. No. Oh, he has motive, means and opportunity as the saying goes, but I somehow can't see that lad as a murderer."

"Anyone is capable of it, in the right circumstances. And he has a temper."

"You're being fair. It's not necessary. I'm under no illusion about human nature. But nevertheless, if a man like that snapped and murdered someone - nine times out of ten, he'd confess before we could get the handcuffs out."

Teresa smiled. "I agree. I'll admit, I was a bit surprised at you rushing to charge him."

"Not I, dear lady. Not I. Young Dempsey. He was in charge of the interview, and jumped the fence a bit early. But it's hard to argue with him - like I said we have means, motive and opportunity. So, I let it stand - for now."

"Right. But if anything were to surface that might clear Dan's name - you wouldn't object?"

"I'd be downright interested. So, may I ask…how far have ye got with your own investigation?"

"I don't know what you mean," Mrs. O'Brien replied with dignity. "What makes you think I would be poking around your case?"

"I've met you. Can't imagine you being able to resist frankly." The detective gave a little chuckle. "All I ask it that you'll tell me if you turn up something."

"Of course. I mean, if I *was* to hear something. Accidentally, like." Mrs. O'Brien rolled her eyes at herself. "Oh okay, yes. I was a bit curious, and it did occur to me that we - Michael and I - might be able to help. People tell me things they wouldn't tell a Garda. And customers gossip."

"Aha! I knew it. So have you any nuggets to impart yet?"

"No. Well - actually I wanted to ask you something first. Two things really." She paused, thinking hard. "The first thing is - do you know yet why Pollard was at the cafe that night? Was it to attend the meeting and if it was, why?"

"So far, nothing conclusive. He's no entry in his work diary or on his phone. The meeting is mentioned in a couple of emails, but only in passing. He was aware of it, that's all we can say for certain at the moment. Does it strike you as unlikely that he would attend? After all, he's an interested party."

"He was a pompous ass who rubbed everyone he dealt with up the wrong way. If he'd shown his face that night, I imagine he would have been run out of it. Unless he didn't care and wanted to stick his oar in anyway."

"That's altogether possible, from what I hear of the man."
"Or he came there for some other reason. We were wondering was he lured there?"

Detective Flynn gave a little gurgle. "Lured? That's a bit cloak and dagger."
"He ended up dead," she replied with some asperity. "If we have the dagger, why not the cloak?"

"You have a point. Well, we'll have his phone records tomorrow. Both mobile and landline. Just in case someone deleted their calls or messages. What was the second thing?"
"It's hard to know quite how to ask this but - I know he was a horrible man, very rude and unreasonable. But was he… crooked?"

Silence, followed by another appreciative chuckle.

"Well now. I wish you had joined the force, Mrs. O'Brien, you'd be the Garda Commissioner by now. Yes. Well, to be fair, the firm Brook and Pollard is under a lot of scrutiny at the moment. You've heard of the Special Crimes Squad? They have been sniffing around the entire outfit for a few months now. Pollard getting murdered has put a serious obstacle in their way - in fact, they're itching to take over. All in the strictest confidence, of course, but there's no doubt about it. Brook and Pollard have been involved in some of the worst property deals in modern history."

"Yet...I have a man telling me today that while Pollard was a pain, he was honest."

"Honest? Hmm. I can't see it. Look, there's a limit to what I can divulge but it's nigh impossible that he was unaware of what was happening. His signature's all over documents, he signed cheques...you get the picture."

"And if I were to make an educated guess...Councillor Seamus Molloy is a close associate of both Mr. Brook and Mr. Pollard?"

"Ah here, woman. Are you bugging my incident room or just psychic?"

Teresa smiled smugly. "I'm just observant, Detective. Just observant."

Chapter 7

I t had taken Clara Walsh precisely two hours to track down Liam Pollard's wife from social media to her place of employment. It hadn't been easy - Mrs. Pollard was not one for selfies and photos of nights out and dinner plates - but a combination of ingenuity and perseverance paid off. She discovered that the widow worked for Kitchen Magic, a bespoke design shop that boasted *"We can transform your kitchen into an oasis of fulfillment."*

Clara snorted but she had to admit the glossy website was very attractive, as were the examples of hand-fitted cabinets and state-of-the-art fridges and freezers.

It had been a while since she and Peadair had changed their cabinets, and the counter-top *was* looking a trifle shabby, if you examined it closely.

Maybe it wouldn't hurt to pop in and get a quote, just out of interest.

Kitchen Magic was located near Merrion Square, an area filled with government buildings, museums and very expensive shops. The outside was painted in black and gold, with large show windows. In each of the window spaces was a single item of kitchen decor; in the first, a large refrigerator in dark green and in the other a single kitchen storage unit in a matt blue.

Both stood under a golden spotlight.

Inside, Clara approached a tall young woman with dark hair and a friendly smile. When she inquired after Annmarie Pollard, the saleswoman's face sobered and Clara was informed in hushed tones, "Mrs. Pollard is absent at present…family tragedy…very sad."

"Oh! How awful. Well, it doesn't matter. She was very helpful, you see, and said if I popped in with some pictures of the kitchen…she was going to advise us on what type of cabinets. But never mind, I'm sure you're busy. I haven't an appointment, obviously. I just popped in…oh, that is lovely, that dark wood with the gold fittings…and I hoped she might fit me in."

But of course! Joyce was only too happy to help. An appointment wasn't necessary - and it would be a pity if Clara were to have had a wasted journey. And there were some really interesting options on sale at the moment, such a pity to miss out…

Clara allowed herself to be led to a client seating area, had a cup of really quite good coffee pressed on her and was soon engrossed in a pile of catalogues showcasing the relative virtues of graphite ash and quartz worktops.

"Annmarie said dark wood might make our kitchen look too dark…" Clara murmured.

Joyce examined the photos Clara had brought along with her. "It's not a huge space, but if you want dark cabinets, a light wall and floor will add space. Have you seen our painted range though? Ah yes, look at this - any one of these new shades would be lovely."

Clara murmured agreement then performed a little gasp, and a dismayed expression.

"Oh dear! I've only just realized. Annmarie Pollard. She

mentioned her husband was in real estate…that poor man that was stabbed in town!"

Joyce nodded, her expression wary. "Yes. That's the - well, the family tragedy I mentioned."

"Ah, the poor woman. Well, I hope they catch however was responsible. That walnut is nice, but maybe the painted range is more practical, what do you think?" She chatted away until Joyce had relaxed again - no point in seeming too eager, and sure, it was very interesting to contemplate what a marble counter-top could do for their kitchen.

"I could make up a three D model for you using these photos," Joyce offered. "It would only take a few minutes."

"That would be amazing." Clara looked around her. "I'm so glad you could fit me in. It was busy the last time I was here."

"Oh, was it a Saturday? Annmarie often works Saturdays and we're always busy."

"It could have been, yes."

"Poor Annmarie," Joyce continued, "I think she worked Saturdays because her husband did too. He was always showing clients some building or other, she said. So, it was easier for her to work the same days. Then they both had Sundays and Mondays off."

Clara tutted sadly. "They sound very close."

Joyce glanced at her. "Well - yes, as far as I could see, she thought the world of him. Why, I don't know."

Clara raised an eyebrow. "Ah. He was a difficult man?"

"He was rude, if I'm being honest. Sour. Permanently annoyed, if you know what I mean."

"Ah yes. Not a fan of sour people. I like a bit of fun, and life. My husband isn't very outgoing, you know, but he's very sweet and lots of fun in a quiet way. Couldn't have married a dour, bad-tempered man."

Joyce shook her head. "Oh, I couldn't either. Not that he was bad-tempered, exactly. It was more that he had no sense of humour, very stuffy, very prickly. Always thought we were trying to put on over on him."

"How sad," Clare said sincerely. "That's an awful way to live."

"Annmarie is so nice...Nearly finished, you'll soon see what I mean about a lighter colour...yes, Annmarie is lovely. Very kind. She didn't seem to mind him, though. If anything - well, I think she was sorry for him. Always making excuses for his rudeness. Apparently, he was under a lot of stress in work."

"Maybe that's why he was so difficult," Clara agreed.

"Meh. I've known her for four years or more. He's been the same all that time."

"Takes all sorts I suppose."

Clara judged it wise to let the subject drop. It wouldn't do for Joyce to tell Annmarie a strange woman had been in discussing her late husband's temperament. She turned her attention to the digital display and was soon genuinely engrossed. Joyce demonstrated how much bigger her kitchen could look, not to mention more modern and better organized.

"You'll find it adds greatly to the value of a home, if you should ever sell."

"I must speak to Peadair about it, but do you know what - I think I'm convinced. Print that last design out for me and I'll bring it home for him to look at. And maybe the second one too, with the light green. Give him a choice."

Joyce smiled broadly, and busied herself putting together an information pack, complete with a pricelist and several versions of the potential kitchen.

"And do tell Annmarie a customer was asking after her, I do

55

hope she's okay."

"I will. Although we don't expect her in for a while... apparently, he left quite a mess behind in the business. She's got a lot to sort out."

"Oh no! That happened to a friend of mine, her husband never told her much about the business and when he died, she was left with debts, and inventory that needed to be sold...such a mess."

"No inventory, really, because it's an estate agency. But there's a partner, and he's being very shady. Very uncoop-erative."

"She needs a good solicitor," Clara advised. "I know a lovely girl - Catherine Sweeney. I can leave you her number. Commercial law is her area."

"Oh. Well, why not? I'm sure she has someone but it won't do any harm." Joyce added the number to her phone contacts. "Just in case."

The women parted on the best of terms, and Clara headed home. She had two important tasks at hand - the first, to report back to Teresa O'Brien and the second, to persuade Peadair that a new kitchen would be a timely investment.

* * *

Mai draped herself across the counter in Ashmara Kapoor's boutique, smiling at Setanta Kapoor in what she fondly hoped was a winning and flirtatious manner. She caught a glimpse of herself in one of the many mirrors that lined the walls of the shop unit and winced. She looked less flirtatious and more demented. She decided to try for a nonchalant, mysterious expression instead. She had an uncomfortable feeling that it wasn't entirely successful, but Setanta grinned back anyway.

"So…" She pointed at the display of vintage brooches and other jewellery, "Can I look at that one, the red one?"

"Ah, the ruby pendant of the Dukes of Leinster," Setanta produced a small red costume jewellery necklace, with gold-coloured metal fittings. "A priceless item, Madame. Priceless. Said to be cursed, by the tenth Duchess, with her dying breath. Her husband had disgraced her in public - wore the wrong colour gloves to a society ball - and she succumbed to a fit of the vapours. Spiteful woman, fierce spiteful."

He held it up to the light and sighed. "If you're willing to risk it…"

"I am," Mai snatched it from him and held it up to her neck. "It suits me. Confound the curse, I must have it. Name your price."

"Twenty." Setanta said, adding, "Eighteen for you. It really does suit you?"

"Guineas or pounds?"

"Euros, ya daft bint. It's really vintage, you know. Ninety eighties, Granny said." Eighteen-year-old Setanta and sixteen year old Mai took a moment to acknowledge the incredible age of the artifact. "Imagine that, forty years ago."

"Love it. I'll pop over with the cash later. So how's your granny? Is she nervous about being alone in the shop?"

"My gran? Hah! She's raging, not scared. She was giving out this morning about the Gardaí arresting poor Dan, the landlords raising the rent and threatening people, that creep Molloy sniffing around…and if she caught the murderer, I wouldn't give much for his chances. She'd pull his hair out, she's so angry."

"My mam is terrified, says she won't do any late shifts in the restaurant until he's caught. Mind you, that could just be her way of getting out of late nights, she's always wanted Dad to hire a night manager."

"Well, I don't blame her. You should be careful too, Mai."

"Why? It's not like someone is murdering random people."

"You don't know that."

"Don't I? Look, it's obvious that Pollard was killed for a reason. If it wasn't Dan, someone else with a grudge. Or his sleazy business partner - have you met him yet?"

"No. When did you meet him?"

Mai grimaced. "I haven't been introduced but I heard him talking to Mrs. O'Brien. He's a real piece of work. Thinks people like me - and probably you, too - are lowering the tone of the neighbourhood. And thinks small shops should be cleared out to make room for big brands and department stores."

Setanta tutted sympathetically. "Sure, there's always one like that. Don't let him upset you."

"Did your Gran meet Liam Pollard before he died?"

"Yeah, twice. He came in once pretending he was interested in renting a unit in the area and asking all kinds of questions. Then he came back a week later, telling her that they were raising the rent."

"What did she do?"

"Told him to get stuffed. She's fairly sure they can't raise it, at least not as much as they want to."

"Oh, that's good news."

"Hmm. It all mounts up though. Overheads are high enough without the rent going up. It's harder and harder to stay afloat. If we went online, it would be easier. "

"Ah no! People would miss coming in."

"Gran would miss her customers, too. But it might come to it yet."

Mai shook her head. "They're ruining everything. *Fancies* will close too, I suppose, and the Bald Bear."

"Paddy says he isn't bothered at all. His lease is airtight according to him and he won't give in without a fight. Hey- there's a thought! Maybe Paddy sneaked into the cafe and bumped him off." Setanta was joking but Mai pricked up her ears.

"I can't see Paddy being violent!"

"Not violent, exactly. But he has some temper on him. And he's ruthless when it comes to his precious barber shop. I could see him doing it, sooner than Dan."

Setanta insisted she take her new necklace with her and drop the payment in later. She glanced at her phone - it really was time to get back to her parents' noodle bar and help out. Biting her lip, she paused outside the Bald Bear Barbers and peered in through the large glass front. Paddy was nowhere to be seen, but the receptionist, Delilah, was sitting idly at the front desk, looking bored.

Only Mai knew that Delilah wasn't the girl's real name; she had started life as Joan Murray from a small town in Mayo but as soon as she had been accepted to the College of Art and Design, she had reinvented herself as Delilah. No one from Ballinarrah would have recognized shy, bespectacled Joan with mousy hair in the confident, raven-haired creature that graced the front desk of Dublin's most achingly cool hairdressers. Today she was dressed in black from head to toe, with flashes of purple, but all in soft floaty lace. Doc Martins and a large velvet bow in purple completed the look. Silver pendants in a mix of symbols and animals draped four deep around her neck while a dozen silver bangles flashed in the light on each arm. Delilah glanced up as Mai entered; her usual expression of disdain gave way to a genuinely warm smile.

"Howya, Kid." Even Delilah's accent was undergoing transformation, determined to erase the last trace of country mouse. Today she was trying out tough, inner-city Dubliner. Last week, she had been a drawling, middle class posh girl.

"Hi, Delilah. Have you a minute?"

"Deffo. Sit yourself down."

"Thanks. Delilah, can I ask you something? Have you heard anything about the lease, all the trouble with the new landlords?"

The receptionist looked sympathetic.

"Ah, Mai. Are your parents worrying about it all?"

"A bit. Not for our place, thankfully, but the street won't be the same if there's no small shops."

"I agree, doesn't bear thinking about, but if it helps, Paddy isn't worried. He says his solicitor looked over his lease and it's airtight. It would take something major to force him out. Like, he'd have to be found with drugs on the premises, that kind of thing."

Mai filed this away for future musing. "That's good, maybe it's the same for the Kapoors."

"Yeah, the only ones really in trouble are Dan and Denise, cos their lease is up for renewal next year. So, yeah, they could be forced out. Paddy says -" Delilah stopped short and reddened. "Ah, I shouldn't be repeating it. But he said that's why Dan did it, if he did it. But he really doesn't think he did it."

"I know what you mean. It does all point to poor Dan. But I don't think he did it either."

60

* * *

Catherine smiled at her secretary and handed him a file.

"All done, Phil. Stick it with the rest."

Phil rolled his eyes. "I'll file it away carefully, like I usually do. For a brilliant legal mind, you've not a trace of organizational skills."

"G'won outta that." She stretched and leaned back in her office chair. It had been a very busy morning and she had been hunched over for the last hour, peering over the terms of a hundred-year-old lease. The owner had stored it in a shoe box, in the back of a wardrobe resulting in yellow, spotted paper and faded ink. Her eyes ached from squinting, but her careful, methodical approach had unlocked the secrets of the old document. Now, a very satisfied client was about to hear that the old building was still hers to sell.

It was time to take a break; she had the chords and lyrics to the new set list for the Super Ukers in her handbag. Even when she couldn't have the ukulele in her hands to strum, she loved to familiarize herself with the chords, making the shapes with her fingers on an imaginary instrument as she hummed along.

Looking at the list reminded her of the conversation in O'Brien's music shop. She had already had a chat with the senior partner in the firm of Boyle, Muckross and Leary. He had agreed that she could take on the West Stephen Street leases as a Pro Bono case, as long as it didn't interfere with her current case load. She could at least prevent the shops being squeezed too much before the leases were up - the rent *could* be raised every 12 months, but it only in line with the current rate of inflation. At present that meant an increase of only 1.5%, and the proposed new rates were in violation of that rule.

Not that it helped *Fancies*, as all the new owners had to do was wait until the lease expired and then raise the rents above the agreed limit.

"They could, of course, try to break the leases with the other tenants," she mused. "But it would be hard. Respectable, hard-working shop owners don't tend to indulge in anti-social behaviour. It's not like they'll be throwing all-night parties or something." Still, an uneasy feeling was nagging at her. Possibly because she knew more than anyone else that Brook and Pollard had an increasingly unsavoury reputation.

On impulse she buzzed Philip and asked him to bring her all the leases for the affected tenants. Pouring over them again, she made a list:

Anti-social behaviour, behaviour likely to bring disrepute, illegal activity, alterations to the structure of the building without permission, breaches of health and safety -specifically anything likely to cause harm to the structure or the tenants -all the ways a lease could be rendered invalid apart from non-payment of rent.

Catherine strummed a few imaginary chords from her favourite Irish song, She Moved Through The Fair. Few Ukulele groups attempted Irish music, preferring the standard popular music but the Super Ukers were determined to add a few to their new repertoire. She loved the challenge and while the traditional keys for Irish music were D and G, she had worked to transpose the famous song to suit the GDAE ukulele tuning.

"T'will not be long love, until our wedding day..." She warbled in her sweet, high voice.

Behind the gentle singing, her mind whirred away. Liam

Pollard had asked a lot of questions about the tenants of Stephen Street West before he ever approached them.

Had he been trying to gather some kind of ammunition to use against them?

* * *

When he wasn't treading the boards as the star Tenor player of the Super Ukers, Eamonn worked in a software company. Binary Worrier Ltd was the brainchild of one of his friends and it specialized in training software engineers in the newest coding and website building techniques. He loved it, working anything from a week to six months in different companies, helping the software department step up to the cutting edge in their industries. The regular change of scene suited him and a happy side effect was that he had built up a network of friends and acquaintances in every aspect of the tech sector in Ireland.

Eamonn thought hard about which of his contacts might be able to help. One name sprang to mind - John Sullivan, known to his mates as Sully, a talented programmer but also a man with a chequered past.

"Eamonn!" John sounded pleased to hear from him. "How's life treating you?"

"Can't complain. Well, I could but if I do, no one listens so I don't bother."

Both men laughed. "Still the same, I see."

"And how are you, John?"

"I'm grand. Business is going well. Maya and the kids are all well. Life is good."

"I'm glad to hear it," Eamonn said, and meant it. Sully had come up the hard way, brighter than most but with few opportunities.

He had taught himself to code but had turned his talents to a life of crime. White-collar crime, which was ironic according to Sully himself, considering he was a proud, working-class boy.

Eamonn had met him when Sully was fresh from a stint in prison, and took a chance on him, giving him his first straight job. Sully had thrived once he was given an opportunity.

"Sully, I need to find out who's behind a holding company - if that's even the correct term. Honestly, I haven't a clue, but I thought you might know how to go about it. There's a company called Southside Developments. When I look them up on the Companies Registration Office website, the directors are listed but I can't find out anything beyond their names and a company address. What's my next move?"

Sully laughed. "Your next move is leaving it to me. We'll start with one of the professional search companies, they'll yield more information including credit reports. I take it you googled the names, checked social media?"

"The names are really common - Peter Murphy, for example - and while there's loads of Peter Murphy's online, there's nothing tying any of them to Southside."

"Ah. That's interesting. Usually, a reputable director of a company makes sure you know they are on the board. It's a badge of pride, if you know what I mean. But if I was to make a fake company, or a shell company, I would use the most generic names possible."

"But they can't be fake names, surely. You have to provide passports and photo ID when you register a company."
Sully snorted. "And there's never been a fake passport made in the whole history of Ireland?"

It was Eamonn's turn to snort. "Well, I suppose ..."

"They don't even have to be fake names," Sully added. "Look, say I want to make a board of directors for a company, I approach a few mates that have common names and a need for ready cash. They sign the paperwork, in exchange for a lump sum. Or I use family members. Or like I said, I create fake IDs."

"Okay. Well, if you can figure it out, I'll be really grateful. Southside are causing a lot of problems for some friends of mine - I'd love to know what we're dealing with."

He could hear the click-click of Sully's fingers already flying over the keyboard.

"Give me a couple of days and I'll know their names, addresses and what they had for breakfast."

* * *

Most people thought of Peadair as a quiet man, especially when his wife Clara was around. She tended to be the one people noticed, and Peadair was well aware that some people laughed up their sleeves at him. There was a very expressive Irish phrase, "*A right gom,*" that meant a gormless, easily led man. He'd heard it whispered in the Golf Club one night, when Clara was elected Captain. When she was made chairperson of the local Residents Association, he knew one or two of the neighbours rolled their eyes at him, calling her bossy and him a soft auld eejit.

Peadair didn't care.

Since Clara was elected Captain of the Golf club, she immediately implemented the Golf Ireland guidelines and made female and male members equal. She initiated a programme to get new blood into the club - youth members from the local schools but also people who perhaps thought of the sport as a snobby, elitist pursuit. She persuaded the members to allow reduced fees and even free lessons to encourage new members.

Some people really didn't like that. Some people, in Peadair's considered opinion, could go boil their heads.

And when Clara got her hooks into the Residents Association, a lot of silly rules that made people's lives miserable were immediately discarded. The previous incumbent had a terrible habit of making it known if a family didn't pay their dues - hefty enough fees for maintenance of the green areas, planting trees, environmental clean-ups - all good and necessary but tough if a family was going through hard times. His wife had put a stop to that and instead took the time to talk to the households involved. As she had always said, most people wanted to contribute, and didn't mind paying, but just couldn't afford it right at that moment. Soon, late fees trickled in, and no one felt publicly humiliated.

Peadair was a shy man, but a strong one. He knew Clara relied on him, that her garrulous prattling was a cover for her own shyness, that she got enthusiastic and carried away at times, and it was his job to gently curb her more extravagant ideas.

Few people realized that Peadair was, in his own field, considered a force to be reckoned with. The University Hibernia history students had voted him "Best Lecturer" five times running. His rebuttal of a certain English historian's take on the "Irish Question" had been published in every leading newspaper and quoted by the President of Ireland. His reputation as a tough but fair professor meant that students worked hard for him, and the most successful had a habit of mentioning him in the dedications and acknowledgments of their first published works.

Peadair loved Clara, his history department, his students and music. He learned to play the ukulele from YouTube videos, sitting in his little office in the university, strumming and singing quietly but would never have had the courage to join a group of actual people, playing in real life, if Clara hadn't taken charge. The ukulele group had given them a better social life, friendship and happy hours belting out their favourite songs.

Mrs. O'Brien had sold him his first ukulele (and his second, third, fourth and fifth - Ukulele players tended to become ukulele collectors very quickly.) He was very fond of the old woman, and the shop. And as a historian he despised the current trend of sweeping away the old to build bland, generic boxes. Dublin was a city steeped in history, with the past and present rubbing along comfortably together. It didn't do to let one side get the upper hand over the other.

"How are you going to find out anything about that Brook fellow?" Clara had asked. "I didn't know you knew anyone in property development."

Peadair had just smiled, which Clara knew meant he was confident of his ground.

And now, sitting in front of him, was his past student, Ronan Mac Manus, who had been on the borderline between a very good two-one degree, and a first. It was his recommendation that had tipped the balance, and he knew Ronan was aware of it.

Mac Manus had not, as it turned out, opted for a career in academia. But the first-class degree had placated his father, the famous owner of Mac Manus Construction. Patrick Mac Manus had not approved of his son's desire to study History and English instead of Business. Ronan had worked himself almost into a breakdown, trying to impress his father and in Peadair's opinion, had more than earned his final grade. Patrick was still not terribly happy that Ronan had defied him for three years, but he enjoyed boasting to his cronies that his son had a First from Ireland's most prestigious university.

"Professor!" Ronan, now a successful young man in his early thirties, shook his hand and seated himself opposite, leaning his arms on the old oak desk.

"Well, no need to ask you how you're doing," Peadair smiled. "You're looking well!"

"I am well, thanks. I'm back working with Dad, we're doing a huge development over in Finglas. How's Clara?"

"She's great, thanks."

They spent a half hour in happy reminiscence and catching up, before Peadair introduced the topic at hand.

"Lovely as it is to see you, Ronan, I must admit to having an ulterior motive. I'm sure you will have heard about a proposed development in West Stephen Street?"

Ronan's expression changed. "Ah. Yes, I have heard rumours." He hesitated. "Please tell me you haven't invested in it?"

Peadair snorted. "No, no - nothing like that."

"Oh, good. That's a relief. What do you want to know?"

"Everything," Peadair grinned. "Starting with the firm of Brook and Pollard, self-styled Commercial Property Experts!"

Chapter 8

Teresa was glad to see Denise opening *Fancies* for business - not only could they not afford to be closed, but it would also do her good to have something to focus on. Dan had finally been released on bail, late the previous evening, but he had gone straight home to the house he shared with his elderly mother. Denise had rung to tell Teresa, the hurt palpable in her voice.

"He wouldn't let me come over, he said there were journalists and that his mother was too upset for visitors."

"Very sensible of him," Mrs. O'Brien had replied briskly. "He's only thinking of you, Denise. And he probably needs some time to process everything that has happened."

"I suppose." Denise hadn't sounded very convinced.

However, the woman opening up the cafe was a different creature from the sad, defeated person on the phone. Defiance radiated from every line of her as she wrenched the shutters up. She turned the key in the lock as if it had personally offended her and the way she set out the blackboard with that day's specials on it, was an act of war.

Mrs. O'Brien fully approved.

"Denise!" she called down the street to her. " How are you?"

"Fine!" Denise waved at her. "Call in when you're free?"

It was an hour before Teresa could make her way to the cafe, the morning had been fully occupied with deliveries and chasing down people to collect their repairs. It never failed to amaze her, how many people left in their instruments for repair begging for a quick job, swearing they needed it for the very next week, but then failed to collect them after Michael had pushed himself to the limit to do them in time. It had been the same in her late husband's time. Once a fortnight, she would sit down with the repair book and start ringing those who had left instruments in for repair ninety days previously.

She was very ready for a coffee and a cake.

No sooner did she appear in the cafe, than Denise ran to greet her. There were two young people waiting on the tables, and Denise had positioned herself in Dan's usual spot behind the counter. Pushing past some tourists who were dithering over which of the cakes to buy, she grabbed Teresa's arm and pulled her to one side.

"Are you free this evening? I am calling a meeting of WE SIT. Alice says we can have it in one of the function rooms in the St. Stephen." The hotel was at the very end of West Stephen Street, a good place to get all the local business owners together.

"The protest group? Really? Is that - well, is that a good idea?" Mrs. O'Brien asked.

"It's a flippin' brilliant idea," Denise snapped. "Dan might be ready to give up, but I'm not. WE SIT needs to reconvene, we need to stand up to the developers and that Brook fella, no matter what happens with the investigation."

"You're right. We can't let them win."

"Maybe someone murdered Pollard solely to derail us," Denise added. "Or maybe it was just coincidence, but if we don't get back on track there'll be no cafe for Dan to come back to - and I won't let that happen."

"Good woman! Well, count me in. I'll round up Michael, and we'll both be here."

Michael was happy to agree. In fact, the young Luthier was in a suspiciously good mood, in her opinion.

"What has you grinning like a big eejit?"

He blushed. "I took your advice and asked Lisa out for a picnic. We're meeting up on her next free Sunday and going to the Phoenix Park." Dublin's biggest park was home to the President of Ireland, Dublin Zoo and a herd of beautiful wild deer. It was a lovely place for a day out, Mrs. O'Brien thought.

"I'm going all out," Michael confided. "I've ordered a picnic hamper, and I'm going to get cushions and blankets and stuff."

"Well done. Life's too short to sit on the sidelines, Michael. And Lisa is too great a catch to expect her to sit around waiting for you to make a move."

He rolled his eyes, but she knew he knew she was right.

Mai called in on her way home from school.

"I've got to work a shift this evening," she said, "But the auld folks will be over to the meeting. And I've been thinking a lot about what Delilah said…that the only way they can break the leases is to prove the tenants were in breach of some rule. The more I think about it, the more convinced I am that was why Pollard was sniffing around before meeting everyone."

"That's very possible, Mai, good thinking. He may even have crept into *Fancies* that night trying to find something."

"Maybe holding a public meeting was against the lease?"

Teresa stared at her. "You know, that's a good point. I'll ask Catherine, she would know."

"When are the Super Ukers reporting back to you?"

"I don't know, but I expect it will take some time. We'll

organize a proper meet up when they do, compare notes."

Mai slung her schoolbag over one shoulder. "Let me know."

"I will," Teresa promised the girl. Left alone again, she sat and had a good hard think about everything. So many threads, she thought, and so many possibilities. One thing they seemed to have overlooked slightly was the involvement of the local council in all this. Councillor Molloy had been very visible at the scene, but she would bet good money that there had been another Councillor there - the woman in the inexpensive suit, who had looked worried. Acting on a hunch, she pulled up the website of the City Council and navigated to the page listing all the elected representatives of the city.

Each name listed had a matching head-shot, Seamus Molloy leering out at her in a professional, studio portrait. Some of the other politicians had similar shots, but most of the pictures were more like awkward passport photos, and among them she found a dark-haired, earnest looking woman. She instantly recognized her as the woman she had seen in the crowd that Friday night.

"Michelle Costello" Teresa read aloud.

"Who's that?" Michael's voice behind her made her jump in fright.

"Oh, for the love of - I didn't hear you come down."

"Sorry," He didn't look a bit sorry, grinning cheekily. "So, who's that?"

"That, my lad, is a Councillor who was also present at the unfortunate events of last week."

He whistled slowly. "Okay. I didn't realize anyone but Molloy was there." He peered closer. "C'mere to me. Doesn't she look a bit familiar?"

"I thought so at the time, but maybe we know the face from

election posters?"

"No, no. That's not it." He clicked his fingers and exclaimed, "Yes! Handmade Stamitz, 2005, red case and a French- no, I tell a lie, a German Dorfler bow."

Mrs. O'Brien stared at him, then comprehension dawned. "Oh - she's a customer?"

"Well, yes and no. She came in a few months ago, we were mad busy, the weekend of the Feis Ceoil."

The Feis was a huge event for classical musical students, who competed yearly for medals. It was a frantic week for the music shop, as students needed their violins and cellos tuned, strings replaced, and so on.

"I don't remember her," Teresa said.
"Ah, but you will. She wanted to leave her violin in for a new set of strings, but she planned on playing it that night - at a trad gig in the Auld Cobbler, she said. She plays folk music and traditional music, mainly. I explained that a new set would go in and out of tune so much, it wouldn't be a good idea. She was okay about it, but just as she was leaving…"
"That big oaf of a man stood on her foot and she screamed like a banshee!" It all came back to Teresa suddenly. "She was in agony! And the language out of her - with a shop full of kids."

"Yes, that's her!"

"Michael, we need to talk to her - she could be our "in" to the council, and what Molloy is up to."

"I have an idea - why don't we email her with an offer? Like, special offer on Spirocore strings. That's what she wanted, if I recall correctly." Michael often couldn't remember where he'd put his keys or where he was supposed to be that day, but an instrument, it's accessories and its repair history he could recall at a moment's notice.

"Say, a reduced price for the set plus free fitting, if she calls into the shop. Then we can get her chatting without it being too awkward."

Teresa admired his sneakiness. "I didn't know you had it in you, but that's genius. Pure devious. Okay, let me at it - with any luck she'll hot-foot it in. Politicians love a bargain."

She fired off the email to Michelle Costello and then composed another one. This was for Finbar O'Leary, the famous traditional musician.

"Dear Finbar,

I hope you don't mind me picking your brains like this, but do you by any chance know a Michelle Costello? She's a DCC Councillor, and a traditional Irish fiddle player. I believe she plays a few gigs in pubs like The Auld Cobbles, so she is reasonably good. If you do know her, would you mind giving me your opinion? We need to approach her about the Business Association here.

Kind regards, Teresa O'Brien."

She didn't have long to wait. Finbar replied first -

"Hey, Teresa.

The mandolin is still going great! Played it at the gig last night and it sounded better than ever. I'll be recording with it next month so might get young Michael to cast his eye over it again, if he doesn't mind. He did a great job, but (don't tell him) I still miss Cathal. No one could make an instrument sing like your late husband.

As for Michelle Costello, as it happens I do know her. She plays a mean fiddle, Donegal style, strong bow arm. Lacks something - technically very, very good but you know me. I prefer a few mistakes and more joy in playing. Still, she's a reliable session musician. Seems very dedicated as a city representative and as far as I have heard, is really into the preservation of Dublin's architecture and culture. Gave a speech about it last year, you'll find it reported

online I'm sure.
  Let Michael know I'll be in soon,
  yours Finbar"

Interesting, Teresa thought. It sounded like Ms. Costello might be key to figuring out parts of the puzzle. No sooner had she thought this, than her inbox showed a reply from the woman herself.

"Dear Mrs. O'Brien
  Thanks for including me in your promotion. I use Spirocore strings and would love to avail of the offer. When would suit for me to call in? I have my fiddle with me today, as it happens and could be in around three?
  Also, my private email is michelleC@irishmailing.ie - rather than using my DCC email, thanks.
  regards, Michelle."

The instruction to use her personal email in future struck her as interesting. Very particular about keeping personal and work emails separate. Mrs. O'Brien made a mental note of it. She wondered if Seamus Molloy would be as conscientious.

Michael was delighted with the result of his little ruse, and insisted on being downstairs in the office area from five minutes to three o'clock. "I'll change her strings in here, and I'll be able to earwig on the conversation."

"Don't be too fast about it," Teresa advised. "I'll need time to get her talking and I don't want to spook her by bringing up the development next door too quickly."

"I'll give you plenty of time," he promised, "And I'll make notes if she says anything interesting."

At three on the dot, the door jangled open, the old bell ringing as a slim, dark-haired woman walked in, carrying a red violin case from the famous french case makers, BAM. She wore a suit, similar to the one she had worn to the WE SITS meeting, and a neatly pressed, crisp white shirt. Her hair was tied back, fastened in place with a plain brown clip. The overall effect was of professionalism.

"Mrs. O'Brien?" She placed her violin case on the counter. "My name is Michelle Costello, you emailed me earlier about a special offer…"

"Of course!" Teresa beamed at her. "I'm so glad you've decided to take us up on it. We don't often have a promotion on Spirocore strings." She wasn't above a little subterfuge in the cause of justice, but she preferred to be as truthful as possible. "In fact, you're our first taker!"

"Well, it was great timing for me. I've been meaning to change them for months now. I did call in a while back, but the young chap said it wasn't a good idea to change them so close to a gig."

"You need a week, at least, to play them in," Teresa was on familiar ground and launched into an explanation about string types and their various properties. She carried the violin into Michael and returned to chat to their customer, trying to think of a way to move from violins to murder without sounding either ghoulish or mad.

As it turned out, Michelle herself raised the subject.

"I saw you last Friday - outside the cafe, when that poor man was killed."

"Oh. Yes, that was dreadful. You were there?"

"Oh yes. I was determined to attend, it's vital to support small business against these big landlords. But by the time I arrived -

well, you know yourself. Do you mind me asking - I heard you were the one to discover the body?"

"Yes. Unfortunately. Michael and I were first to arrive you see, and we found it - him - lying there."

"Oh, that must have been awful. I didn't like the man, in all honesty but no one deserved to die like that."

Teresa's ears pricked up. "You knew poor Mr. Pollard?"

"Professionally, not personally. I've crossed paths with him several times over local planning issues, and of course, their treatment of tenants. I know one shouldn't speak ill of the dead but the way his firm carried on was a disgrace."

"Really? Like, illegal stuff or just sharp practice?"

"We-ell, I couldn't go so far as to say illegal. No. But definitely unscrupulous. Brook, I've met once or twice, and he didn't seem too bad. But Pollard - well, I wouldn't put anything past Liam Pollard."

"I've met Mr Brook," Teresa volunteered. "He came to do a valuation on this building for me, quite recently."

"Did he? Well, you'll probably be safe enough with him. I got the impression it was Pollard who drove the bus, so to speak. He seemed to be in charge, Brook was more of a "yes man," in that set up."

"What do you make of the situation next door?"

"It's bad. Southside seem determined to drive out the tenants and to be honest, I can't see that there's much anyone can do about it. There's talk of turning the entire building into a department store - some big names being mentioned. Of course, Councilor Molloy has a finger in that pie, so - he tends to get his own way."

"You don't sound very hopeful! Are we wasting our time trying to fight this then?"

"Oh, no - don't get me wrong," Michelle said earnestly. "It's very important to stand up to them. If nothing else, it'll delay them. And if they think they are going to meet with robust opposition, they'll start offering compensation to the tenants. Better than being turfed out with nothing. Sometimes that's all we can do."

Teresa nodded. "I suppose, although it's a bit depressing to think they might get away with it."

"Oh, look, sure I know! And I'm not saying give up just yet. Far from it. But sadly, I've a lot of experience in these matters. Everything is weighted on the side of the developers, especially with certain types on the council and the planning board."

"Oh. I've heard people saying - well, not to mention names, but that there are some councilors with vested interests, shall we say?"

"Hah. I don't mind mentioning names, Seamus Molloy, for example. That man is a menace. He's hand in glove with every developer, if he had his way they'd pave over the park and build an apartment block on it!"

Teresa laughed. "Well, it was his name that I heard. I take it, it's true then. I suppose we'd be wasting our time asking him for help?"

"Him! He'd be as much use as a chocolate teapot. But I might be able to help, if you like?"

"I'd really appreciate that. We're having another meeting tonight - in the St Stephen Hotel, this time. It didn't seem right to use *Fancies*."

"What time?"

"Half past six, would that suit you?"

"Yes. It might be seven before I get there, but I'll do my best. I've a pack with handy information that I can bring - phone numbers, legal advice, anything that might help. I'll bring some along."

Teresa was impressed. "Lovely. Thanks so much, Michelle, your presence will mean a lot to people."

Michael appeared behind her, bearing the old fiddle with its new set of strings. "I've tuned it up, and if you play and tune it regularly over the next few days it will soon settle in. It's sounding well, in my opinion. You had a lot of resin on the bow, though."

It was a constant source of irritation to the young Luthier that traditional player would insist on loading the bow with so much resin it made a harsh squeaky sound. He added sternly, "I removed the build-up of old resin dust from around the bridge too. It doesn't help the sound, and it's bad for the varnish."

Michelle Costello rolled her eyes. "Oh my god, did he learn that from Cathal O'Brien? He used to give me the same lecture when I was a kid."

"You should have listened to him then," Michael muttered, but at a sharp glance from Mrs. O'Brien, he fixed a smile on his face and said, "Ah well, sorry, it's a bugbear of mine."

"And Ms. Costello has volunteered to come to the protest meeting tonight, Michael, isn't that kind of her?"

"Absolutely, thanks very much," but he didn't sound very enthused. Michelle didn't seem to notice, thankfully and departed in high good humour, Teresa walking her to the door and waving her off. Once the woman had taken her leave, she turned to Michael in exasperation.

"Honestly!"

"What? I was right. She's ruining her bow hair and making a mess of her violin. Why on earth won't they listen when we tell them it's not good practice?"

"Because that's what traditional Irish fiddlers have done for years, and nothing will change their minds. You know this, Cathal knew this, and yet ye lecture them every single time!"

"Well, I hate to see a good bow ruined."

"And I would hate to alienate possibly the only councilor who gives a flying fiddlers about this street and our neighbours. We're lucky she didn't take offense and change her mind about coming tonight."

"Well, Denise will be delighted." Michael said. "And I suppose her heart is in the right place, if she's willing to help." But he still went upstairs muttering about people ruining good bows.

Teresa rolled her eyes. Sometimes Michael reminded her so much of her late husband!

Chapter 9

Teresa was surprised to hear from Clara so quickly. A text had popped up on her phone as she sipped her afternoon coffee (and munched on a honey cake- after all the meeting would make her late for her dinner and she needed to keep her strength up.)

Clara's text ran:

Lots to tell you, be in later to fill you in. I'm getting a new kitchen fitted so will be after four. Also need four sets of Aquila Lava Strings for Concert Uke. Do you think lavender good choice for walls?

Teresa blinked at the screen. Surely, Clara couldn't have gone into Kitchen Magic and actually ordered a new kitchen? But then again, it was Clara…She wondered if Peadair would ever forgive her for letting his wife within ten feet of Dublin's most expensive kitchen designers!

She wondered if the irrepressible Clara had actually found out anything or had she just spent the time gossiping and picking out kitchen cupboards. Still, she wouldn't have to wait long to find out.

And hot on the heels of Clara's text was one from Eamonn. Despite the fact that text messages clearly stated who the sender was, he started off by stating -

"Mrs. O'Brien, this is Eamonn."

Teresa sighed. Eamonn thought anyone over fifty was bewildered by technology and treated them like little children, easily confused.

"I've some interesting info on Southside. Will be in later today. Heard there's a protest meeting, can outsiders attend? would like to support."

She texted back...

"Hi Eamonn, this is Teresa O'Brien here. Of O'Brien's Music. In case your phone didn't make that clear. Yes, call in later. Yes, attend meeting, all welcome."

She added as an afterthought:

"Clara calling in at four, maybe call in same time."

If two of her investigative minions were going to pop in at four that afternoon, she thought, why not make it a clean sweep.

She opened her WhatsApp and created a group chat. She hesitated for a moment over what to call it - it didn't seem right to be too frivolous, after all this was a case of murder. But it went against the grain to call it something pompous. After a moment's thought she settled on, "Music Shop group," which was boring but would do.

"Hi everyone," Teresa wrote. "Clara and Eamonn have some news and will be in shop around four pm. If anyone else is free to come in at that time, please do."

She added a smiley face, so it didn't sound too much like an order and sat back with a sigh. It looked like it was going to be a busy day and that was apart from actual customers. Still, maybe they were getting somewhere at last. It would be great to tell Denise some good news at the meeting.

Her reverie was broken by the clanging of the shop door, a group of tourists trooping in shyly. All the way from Japan, armed with guidebooks that mentioned O'Brien's as a must-see part of Dublin history, they were enthralled by the tiny shop and its air of controlled chaos. They were particularly interested in Irish traditional music, and showed her photos of Finbar O'Leary in the shop, playing mandolin. There were quite a few photos online of famous musicians in the shop, from rock stars to classical maestros but they were huge fans of O'Leary's group, The Irishmen. After a happy half hour listening to Mrs. O'Brien's stories, and choosing tin whistles and ballad books, they departed - each in turn taking a photo of the woman herself and promising to post them online.

Teresa laughed as they left. It was always fun to feel like a celebrity, albeit a very minor one, and at seventy plus years of age, rather nice to think young people might put her on their social media.

The tourists were followed by the usual stream of clients, parents buying strings or shoulder rests or trying to figure out what the teacher meant by the scribbled note in the margin of the manuscript copy.

"What's a Tutu mumu?" one mother wailed plaintively. "I've looked online, I've asked all the other parents...no one knows!"

"Mute," Teresa explained. "I'm used to Miss Reilly's handwriting. She means "Tourte Mute," it's for playing quiet passages in some pieces. It fits on the bridge, and when you're not using it, it sits between the bridge and the tailpiece - which is good because they're less likely to lose it! That'll be three euro, twenty cent, please."

Before she realized it, it was four o'clock and Clara arrived, slightly out of breath but in high good humour. Eamonn slipped in behind her, and the pair waited patiently until she finished serving her customers.

"I have so much to tell you," Clara launched into her tale as soon as the last customer exited. "First of all, Kitchen Magic is a lovely shop, I'm so glad I found it. I didn't realize how out of date our kitchen was until I saw their designs and even Peadair saw it in the end, which is great because otherwise it would be hard to explain to him why the kitchen was being pulled apart! Joyce - that's the saleswoman, she's dead sound - Joyce said our new kitchen would add thousands to the value of the house, not that we plan on selling but sure, isn't it *nice* to know that? Joyce is flat out in there, covering for poor Annmarie Pollard. And she told me all about the Pollards - we've had quite a few chats over the last couple of days, because of ordering the new kitchen, which makes it worth the money really, doesn't it? Joyce says Ann Marie is as straight as a die, nothing shady about her and she thinks the world of her. Didn't like Liam Pollard at all, but said she figured there had to be something good in him if Ann Marie liked him."

Clara paused to draw breath. "Anyway, long story short, Ann Marie has been left a very rich woman as a result of Pollard's death, but she is having a great deal of trouble with Brook. Joyce says the widow has asked several times to see the books for the firm, and now has her solicitor chasing them up, and Brook is being extremely uncooperative. He implied to the solicitor that Pollard was up to some very shady dealings and he was trying to protect the widow from the harsh truth - which, I suppose, could be true?" she ended doubtfully.

"That *is* interesting," Teresa replied. "It doesn't rule her out but it does sound as if she wasn't aware of what Brook and Pollard were doing."

Eamonn snorted. "Want to bet? I found out who is behind Southside Development. Four directors, three of whom I don't know much about…yet. But the last one is - Annmarie Pollard!"

Both women gaped at him.

"What?" Clara shook her head. "The woman Joyce described to me would never be mixed up in a shady property deal."

"Well, maybe Joyce doesn't know her as well as she thinks she does."

The argument was cut short by the arrival of Catherine, clutching a folder and looking as ever, more like a tall, willowy pixie than a lawyer. Hot on her heels was Peadair, calm and stoic but with a twinkle of excitement in his eyes.

Teresa brought the new arrivals up to date and was surprised when Peadair immediately spoke up.

"Ah. Well, it's altogether possible that Mrs. Pollard doesn't know she's a director of Southside, or at least doesn't realize the significance. I have some small intel of my own to add," He beamed around proudly. "Brook and Pollard have a reputation for sailing rather close to the wind and it wouldn't be the first time they've "run with the hares and hunted with the hounds," so to speak. In short, they have a vested interest in Southside and they are masquerading as the mere agents when in fact they are…the landlords!"

A gratifying gasp of surprise greeted this nugget of information.

"And, according to my source - young Ronan Mac Manus, Clara, he sends his regards - I've been told that the firm of Brook and Pollard have done this before. Sham companies, filled with directors who don't know or care what the company does, often people related to them - like Mrs. Pollard."

"That's more or less what I was told," Eamonn added eagerly. "But that doesn't mean she didn't know all about it."

"I'm telling you, Joyce says she's an honest, decent woman.

And I believe her. I bet that her snake of a husband got her to sign off on it, without her realizing what they were up to."

"It's not that simple," Catherine said. "To form a company, any party named as director is asked for signatures, declarations, there's a lot of paperwork. It's highly unlikely she didn't know she was being signed up as director of Southside Developments Limited."

"But- that doesn't mean she knew Southside was bullying tenants," Clara pointed out.

"No, you're right," Catherine conceded. "But we have to consider her a person of interest."

"Even if she did know, does that mean she had a motive to murder her husband? She was already a director, she stood to gain financially from the development."

"The same can be said for Brook," Eamonn pointed out. "What's the advantage to him if Pollard dies? Surely it just complicates their scheming?"

"We're missing something," Teresa pursed her lips. "Has anyone else noticed, no two people seem to have the same story about Pollard?"

"I thought everyone was agreed that they didn't like the man?" Peadair replied.

"Yes, yes but - never mind. It's just something that strikes me as odd. Leave it with me. I need to think."

The four ukulele players exchanged glances.

"Well, we'll keep digging and you keep thinking," Catherine said. "But you haven't heard my news yet!"

All eyes turned to the young solicitor.

"I have been going over the leases for next door with a fine-tooth comb. And Mai was right - there are some clauses that would mean the tenants had broken the terms and conditions.

For example, Pollard was asking about all the comings and goings at the Kapoors - well, it's a condition of the lease that only the business listed operates out of the unit. I think he was trying to find out if they were using it for any other purpose. If a landlord wants to be really unreasonable, even selling wholesale instead of retail out of the unit could be construed as "operating" another, unlisted business."

She opened her folder. "Similarly, if Dan and Denise catered for an event, and cooked the food on the premises of Fancies, he could claim the same. In fact, I found out that Brook and Pollard Limited broke a lease in another building, for a cafe, on those very grounds."

"So, could holding a meeting in the cafe have broken the lease?" Eamonn asked.

"I don't think so, but he might have thought he could spin it some kind of way. Or that he could frighten Dan into thinking it was enough. I've been reading up on some recent judgments and to be honest, it's a grey area. If he made out it was a political party meeting, maybe he could break the lease. It's very unlikely, in my opinion. Any decent lawyer could fight it. But that doesn't mean he wasn't there looking for something."

"It would explain why he attended the meeting!" Clara interjected.

"Does it?" Teresa was not convinced. "I wonder. I do think it's the explanation for him hanging around over the last few weeks. I'm just reluctant to assume that's why he was there last Friday."

"Do you still think he was lured there?"

"I'm really not sure. We'll keep an open mind on that one. I need to find out more about him, I think. There are too many things not quite adding up." She looked around at the others.

"You've all done amazingly well. I wish Mai and Michael were here to hear all this, but if you each can write up a short summary and post it in the WhatsApp group, we can make sure everyone is in the loop."

"I love that we have our own group," Clara remarked happily. "I like the idea of us being the Music Shop Sleuths."

"The Super Uker Sleuths," Eamonn suggested.

"Mai isn't a Super Uker, Eamonn but she's even more involved than we are. No, it should be the Music Shop."

"How about the Music Shop Musketeers?" Peadair liked a literary twist to a title.

They exited, promising to be back in time for the meeting at six thirty, and Mrs.O'Brien could hear them bickering gently as they wandered off to get food. Minutes later the door opened and Mai stuck her head in.

"Howya! The others are over in the Noodle Palace, they're going to fill me in on the latest developments. You catch Michael up, before the meeting. And I've some gossip too - I wanted to tell you in person. I got talking to a girl in school whose dad works in the planning section. Seamus Molloy has been talking a lot about the West Stephen Street businesses, trying to get support for a large-scale development. But the good news is, her dad is dead set against it, and so are a lot of people. She's going to tell him about WE SIT and the protest and fingers crossed, we'll have some allies in the planning office who can help."

"That's excellent news, Mai. Well done."

The teenager looked absurdly pleased at the praise. "Anything to help, Mrs. O'Brien. See you later!"

All that was left to do now was debrief Michael on the latest events, lock up the shop and get down to the St. Stephen Hotel, ready to cause trouble for the greedy landlords of Dublin City.

Chapter 10

"First order of business," Denise said loudly, straining to be heard over the excited chatter of the assembled business owners and their supporters, "First order of business is to elect a committee. To this end, I propose myself, Ashmara Kapoor and Paddy Clancy to represent the business owners." A general murmur of approval swept through the crowd. "I would like to ask for three of the residential tenants to put themselves forward to represent their interests."

She looked around hopefully, but at first no one made any move to volunteer.

"Come on, people! If you are a tenant of any of the apartments this proposed development is just as bad for you, as it is for us shop owners."

A young woman, dressed in a colourful suit with a matching Hijab, stood up shyly. "I don't mind offering," she said. "I'm Nadia, and I live at apartment fifty-nine."

"Excellent, thank you. Anyone else?"

A tall lad, who looked to be about nineteen, dressed in a Galway jersey, stood up. "I'm Ben, Ben Dunphy and I live with my brother Aidan in apartment twenty." A round of applause from the crowd made the young man blush a deep crimson. Nadia gave him an encouraging thumbs up.

An older man, dressed in a suit, stood up. "I'm Alan Corr and I live in number seventy, so that's one from each floor. I'm happy to volunteer, if you'll have me."

Denise clapped her hands.

"That's just perfect. Now, I have one more proposal. To represent the rest of West Stephen Street, and to act as our leader and I suppose, figurehead, I propose Mrs. O'Brien, from O'Brien's Music Shop. Most of you know, she is our streets longest serving business-person. No one can speak more eloquently about the area than she can."

Another round of applause greeted this, and people began to call out, "Absolutely!" and "Hear Hear!" Michael was even heard to go "Whoo Hooo!" much to Teresa O'Brien's embarrassment.

Feeling rather ambushed, but deeply flattered all the same, she stood up and said, "If you think I can be of any use…" which just made people cheer a bit louder.

"Okay, everyone, simmer down!" Denise held her hands. "Can the new committee please make its way to the top of the room please, and sit down. Now, would anyone of ye like to volunteer to take minutes?"

Nadia held up her hand. "I've got a pen and notebook, I'll take everything down."

"Right then. Let's call this meeting of WE SIT to order."

An expectant silence fell over the audience.

"There's something we should address right away." Denise's voice rang out firmly and defiantly. "I see some members of the Press are here tonight - and much as I'd like to think it is out of interest for our plight as we battle predatory landlords, we all know it's because of the tragic events last week. So let me say this, and then we can move on to the main business -

Dan Riordan did not harm that unfortunate man, in any way. And anyone who says differently is a liar. I know he's innocent, and I expect this to be proven very soon. Liam Pollard was not a friend to the businesses on this street, but no one deserves to die like that, and I hope the Gardaí solve this crime as soon as possible and bring his killer to justice. But that person is not Dan, and all of you who know him, know I'm right!"

Another cheer went up at this, and thunderous applause rang out for several minutes. The journalists present were either scribbling frantically or recording on their phones, depending on their age bracket. Denise went pink but remained standing, head held high.

"I now call upon our new chairperson, Mrs. Teresa O'Brien, to start this meeting."

Teresa stood up, and patted Denise on the shoulder. "Well said," she whispered.

To the audience, she said, "Good evening, everyone, and thank you all for attending. Our new committee will need all the help you can give, this is a fight that needs everyone united and involved. I would like to invite the journalists present to remain, because this is a story worth reporting. This is a battle for the heart - the soul, even - of our beloved city. Do we want to preserve our tradition of unique, individual shops? or do we want to see it become yet another generic high street, filled with soulless, mass-produced goods? I've worked in the music shop since I married Cathal O'Brien, fifty years ago. His father and grandfather also worked on this street, in the same shop. Around us, the landscape has changed - new faces, new shops - but the one thing that never changes is the individuality, the uniqueness, of every business. Grafton Street has the big department stores, the Stephen's Green Shopping

Centre has them too. But in the streets around us are the designers, the craftsmen, the artisan bakers and independent booksellers…and without them, Dublin just won't be the same."

"So, whether you live or work around here, this is your fight. This is where we decide what kind of city we want - a place for everyone, new and old, to express themselves or a boring place devoid of creativity." She glanced at the other committee members. "Let's start by hearing from the tenants of the building, and what they think about the new landlords."

She sat down, feeling a bit giddy. The speech had come from her heart, and she hoped it hadn't come over as too dramatic. But everyone seemed to enjoy it, judging by the response. The residential tenants stood up next, explaining how increased rent meant they would almost certainly have to move, but where to? Rents were inflated across the city and housing security was a major issue everywhere in Ireland. There was a heartfelt cheer when they finished, and Teresa could see the journalists taking notes. Next up was Ashmara Kapoor, who explained the pressures facing small businesses, from spiraling costs to competition with the Internet. She was a good speaker and had the audience laughing ruefully. Paddy came next, explaining how the new landlords had harassed and bullied them, and read out one of the letters he had received from Brook and Pollard Limited. It was rude, unhelpful and made it clear that there was no desire to negotiate.

"See what we're up against?" Denise asked the crowd. "I see Councilor Michelle Costello has arrived, I hope she heard what Paddy had to say! How can you deal with people who are so unreasonable? They want us out, and they don't care how they go about it."

All eyes turned to the local politician, and Michelle waved in return.

"I did indeed hear it, and I am appalled. Like all of you, I'm sick of these greedy developers taking over our city. I for one will be fighting your corner in the Council, no matter how slim a chance we have."

Teresa could see Michael rolling his eyes from the top of the room.

"Ms. Costello," She said, gesturing to the young woman, "Could you tell us, from your experience, what we should be doing next? Who should we contact, who should we be lobbying… that sort of thing?"

Michelle made her way to the top of the room and held a glossy paper folder up.

"This is my resource pack, filled with the names and emails of politicians, the planning board, local press and so on. You should all be contacting them, complaining about what's happening here and making sure they are aware of the problem. I provide sample emails, use them as templates. Avoid bad language or any kind of threat - you don't want to alienate people. You'll also find suggestions for fundraising and so on."

Everyone clapped politely, but it was clear they had hoped for something a little more impassioned. Teresa wondered if they were all being too idealistic, naive even. Michelle certainly seemed to think it was a tough sell. Then again, people liked the idea of protesting but the boring reality of writing emails, fundraising and so on was not as attractive.

"Thanks, Michelle," Denise said. "We really appreciate you attending, and I hope the media takes note of this - we have the support of at least some members of the city council! Now, while we will need to organize a campaign of lobbying government representatives and raising awareness, I suggest that we also start the process of organising a protest march."

Teresa saw Michelle shake her head, just slightly but enough to convey that she considered it a bad move. Denise was oblivious to the Councillor however, and the crowd gave a cheer.

"If they won't negotiate, we need to be ready to escalate the protest and I for one am willing to march on Leinster House!"

From the reaction of the reporters, this made a good hook for their story. Denise winked at Teresa, and raised her arms. "We'll try every means to reach a fair outcome but rest assured - if it's a fight they want, it's a fight they'll get!"

Chapter 11

"Well, that was some meeting!" Mai burst into the shop, excitement all over her face. "Feels like we're really getting somewhere now. Except that Councillor, Costello – she was a wet blanket, wasn't she? Do you know, afterwards when we were all talking about the situation, she actually told Mrs. Kapoor she'd be better off online? She means well, I suppose but it's hardly fighting spirit, eh?"

Teresa agreed. "Yes, she's not exactly hopeful. Still, she told us herself, she's seen this happen over and over. I suppose it's hard to be optimistic when you see these developers get away with it time and again."

"Setanta says it's not all developers, but that the good ones are crowded out by the unscrupulous ones. And Peadair said that friend of his, the one who gave him all the inside scoop on Brook and Pollard – he's all right."

"Ah pet, there are always good people. And we need development, we need progress. That fine building we're trying to save was new once, and not that long ago. People didn't like the old tenements being pulled down to build that, either. But that gave housing, and businesses to the street. This new development will make lots of people homeless and put half a dozen people out of work. What good is that?"

"Don't have to convince me, Mrs. O'Brien. It's bad for the city, bad for the environment and bad for people like the Kapoors. And the others, of course."

Teresa bit her lip. The temptation to laugh at Mai's obvious partiality for a certain Kapoor was almost overpowering. Ah, to be sixteen and in the throes of a first crush again…on second thoughts, no. Her first crush had been on a very unsuitable young man who wore his hair slicked back and affected the most ridiculous outfits. It wouldn't have worked at all.

"Mrs. O'Brien, do you think we can figure out who killed Pollard? Only, we seem to be gathering a lot of information but to be honest, I haven't a clue what to do with it all."

"That's the first step, Mai. Information is vital. We need to understand the situation, know all the moving parts, see where it all fits together. Otherwise, we're just guessing. The more we know, the more we can rule someone in – or out. Take Dan, for example. If we didn't know him, and Denise too, we could easily believe he was capable of murder. But we know he's really gentle underneath, we know Denise would never defend a murderer, we know she knows him best – oh!"

"What is it?" Mai eyed her expectantly.

"Nothing. Something. I need to think about it." She whipped out her phone, opened Samsung Notes – thanks to her granddaughter, and her many lessons in modern technology – and quickly typed in a few words. "There, that'll remind me."

"You're amazing, Mrs. O'Brien. And a bit scary."

"Scary?"

"Yeah, all my mates think so. It's not normal, someone your age being able to use Facebook and Insta and all those things. But in a good way, don't be offended! Like, you're bad-ass."

Teresa sniffed. She wasn't entirely sure whether to rebuke the teenager for cheek or be flattered. She settled for a harrumph and a change of subject.

"What did your parents think of the meeting?"

"Mam was impressed, she said it's a good idea to start lobbying politicians, really get them on board. Dad was a bit disappointed that there won't be a rally or a march straight off the bat – he used to be a real firebrand back in his college days. He was all ready to chain himself to the railings for the cause."

"What railings did he have in mind?"

"Oh, any handy set. Maybe around Leinster House, or the Stephen's Green, who knows? Oh, and he said to tell you, your speech was great. Which it was, everyone agreed."

"He's very kind, thanks. So, your dad agrees with Denise that we should organize something a bit more direct…he may have a point. It would get a bit of publicity, at any rate."

"Deffo. Will I suggest to him that he volunteer to get that underway? He's itching to get involved."

"Do. Something simple, mind – placards and a petition, maybe. I don't want us on the six o'clock news, being hauled off in handcuffs for disturbing the peace. And make sure he knows, it may not even be needed."

"I can't guarantee anything, but I'll try to keep him in check. And sure, if we win before the march is needed it can be a victory rally. Are you meeting up with the others later?"

Clara had texted earlier to say the Super Ukers were rehearsing in the function room of the St Stephen Hotel from five o'clock and had suggested that maybe she and Michael would like to call down, hear them play and then have a catch up. Teresa explained the plan to Mai.

"Brill, I'll pop over at five then. We'll all go together."

"Mai, don't your parents mind you wandering around with us, at a moment's notice?"

"Of course not. I tell them where I'm going, and when I'll be back and they have a tracker app on my phone. Plus, everyone around here knows me, I can't get away with anything."

Privately, Mrs. O'Brien suspected that Mai got away with a lot more than her parents would ever know, but she had to admit the teenager was a capable, clever young woman, and sensible enough for her age. A hard day's work passed the time quickly, and by five o'clock, she was happy to close up and attend the rehearsal. Michael faffed around for a few minutes past the hour, as ever finding some last minute adjustment needed to a repair, but even he seemed glad to get out of work.

"It's been a long week," he remarked, shrugging on his jacket. "I'll be glad when it's over."

"Where is Mai?" Teresa looked at her watch for the umpteenth time. "It's not like her to be late. She was dying to catch up with the others, earlier."

"She's probably busy in the Noodle Palace," Michael popped his head out the door and peered across the street. "Oh. That's odd. The shutters are down on the restaurant."

"What?" Teresa stepped out of the building and walked a few steps towards the noodle bar. "You're right. How odd."

She glanced around. Kapoors was still open, they shut at six o'clock. *Fancies* normally opened late on a Thursday, until ten p.m. to take advantage of the city's late night shopping evening, but with recent events Denise had been shutting earlier. Still, she was a bit surprised to see the shutters on the cafe half down, leaving a gap of about four feet at the bottom.

"Michael, see if she's in Kapoors." Teresa instructed as she walked briskly towards accents. Michael obeyed, looking worried. She put her hand to the shutters and pulled – they wouldn't budge.

"Electric," she muttered to herself. Reaching beneath the security barrier, she put her hand to the door, and pushed hard. It opened. Bending almost double she went under the shutter, and entered the café. It was in total darkness save for the weak evening light that came through the bit of window not already covered by the security shutter.

"Denise?" She called out. "Are you here? Mai?"

Silence. She was about to turn and leave, wondering if Michael had found anyone in Kapoors, when a tiny groan reached her ears.

"Hello!" She fumbled for a light switch before remembering the torch on her phone. A narrow but very bright beam of light cut through the gloom. Sweeping systematically left to right ahead of her she took one, two, three steps into the interior – and saw a Doc Martin clad foot peeking out from behind the counter.

"Oh no! Mai!" The girl was lying crumpled on the floor, her face streaked with blood and her breathing shallow. "Michael," She screamed as loudly as she could, while dialing the emergency services on nine, nine, nine. "Ambulance, 23 West Stephen Street – café named Fancies…"

"Oh my god!" Michael appeared, Setanta Kapoor beside him. The younger man immediately knelt down, taking Mai's wrist and feeling for a pulse. "Strong," he said. "That's good. Mai! Can you hear me?" The girl's eyes fluttered. "Mai, can you open your eyes?"

To Mrs. O'Brien's eternal relief, Mai obeyed. She looked straight at Setanta and smiled. "Howya."

Setanta let out a long breath. "Howya, Mai. No, don't move.

Stay where you are, there's an ambulance on the way. Can you tell me how many fingers I'm holding up?"

"Give over, Set. You're not even a medical student yet. Mrs. O'Brien – I need to tell you. Denise got a call from Dan, asking her to visit him. She left in a terrible hurry. She asked me to lock up…OW! My head hurts…someone hit me, from behind."

Setanta frowned. "Mai, you shouldn't be stressing."

"I'm not stressing, you big eejit. You're stressing me, telling me what to do."

"Setanta is only trying to help, Mai. But carry on, tell me what happened, nice and calmly." Teresa patted Setanta's arm. "She won't get upset, will you?"

"No. I'm perfectly calm. Except for the pain in my head – they gave me a right whack. Look, before the ambulance comes, or the cops – I promised Denise I'd lock up for her. She put the shutters at half mast and locked the door. I had the spare keys. When my shift ended, that lazy git Niall hadn't arrived yet, so I shut up the Noodle Palace, ran over here and came in to finish closing it up. I was here maybe five minutes, turning off the switches and tidying…then I went to set the alarm…Bang!"

"Where's the patient?" A cheery voice called from the doorway. Two paramedics peered into the gloom. "Can we get some lights on in here."

Teresa stood back while the medics went to work, and Michael found the light switches. Mai submitted meekly to being poked and prodded, obviously feeling a little less robust than she had let on. She was reluctant to go to Accident and Emergency, but the ambulance men insisted, and Setanta volunteered to accompany her.

"Mrs. O'Brien," Mai pressed the keys to both the Noodle

Palace and Fancies into her hand. "Can you close up here, and then let Niall into the Palace, assuming the little brat ever turns up?"

"Of course. And Mai, do your parents have CCTV cameras now?" Mr Khan had been adamant that he would install some after the murder.

"Oh. Yes…they were put in place a few days ago."

"Can I check them?"

"Of course. Oh, and ring my parents please – they'll go berserk if they think I'm seriously injured. They'll believe you."

Teresa saw her safely into the ambulance, smiling as she heard Setanta fussing over the patient as the doors closed. The phone call to Mai's parents wasn't easy; her mother was practical, if upset, but poor Mr. Khan was distraught. He often gave out about Mai but only to hide how proud he was of her and how much he cared. It took her quite a while to calm him down, and only her repeated reassurance that his daughter was talking and alert soothed him. The errant Niall had finally turned up for his shift and she put him to work immediately, her stern manner putting enough fear into the lad so that he actually set to cooking and serving without complaint.

A squad car turned up, two Gardaí ready to take statements and examine the scene. They seemed inclined to treat it as a robbery, despite the fact that the till was untouched and Mai's rather expensive watch and phone both left behind. Teresa bit her tongue; odds were that once Detective Malachy Flynn got wind of the evening's events, he would put a different spin on it. Leave it to him, she thought.

She checked her watch. If she hurried, she might still be in time to catch the end of the rehearsal. Now, more than ever she wanted to sit down and talk things over with the group. But first, she needed to check the footage from the cameras. The Khans had spared no expense, opting for a state of the art, digital recording system – no discs, just a massive hard-drive that stored all the footage and uploaded it to the cloud for backup. Michael shuddered at the sight of the operating system, displayed on a small monitor in the back room of the noodle bar.

"It looks complicated, Mrs. O'Brien. Should we not just turn it over to the Gardaí and let them sort it out?"

"Of course we'll turn it over to them. No doubt someone will call tomorrow and ask Mr. Khan for it. But we're just going to take a sneak peak first."

The camera took in the front of the noodle restaurant, clearly showing both the door to the music shop, the lane way beside it, and the entrance to Fancies. You could also see the shops on either side, but not as clearly. She replayed the last two hours of filming on fast forward, pausing to examine every passerby, and customer, but nothing stood out. They went in, they came out clutching coffee. Groups entered together, stayed half an hour or so, and exited laughing and chatting. She wound it back another hour, and still nothing.

"Go back over the quarter of hour coming up to the attack," Michael advised. They watched like hawks, but after Denise left and crossed the road to the Palace, and Mai crossed back over to let herself in to Fancies…nobody so much as looked in the window of the café.

"Wait!" Michael pointed to the laneway between the music shop and the café. "What's that?"

"Oh." A figure, in a dark top and leggings, face well hidden by the hood of the sweatshirt, paused at the windows of the music shop before ducking into the laneway beside it. "Let's roll on."

They followed the footage until they reached the live view, but the figure never re-emerged.

"It's possibly nothing…someone going the back way into the apartments or something. Assuming there is a back way in."

"You're probably right, Michael. But it's the only lead we've got. I wonder – no one saw anyone enter *Fancies* on the night of the murder either, not after Denise left."

"There's no way in from the laneway, we know that."

"Do we? We assumed that. But there is a back door to the cafe, from that little yard where they store their bins."

"But it's impossible to get into the yard from anywhere but the café," Michael pointed out.

"So we think. Anyway, let's go meet the Super Ukers. We need to get to the bottom of this, my lad. Hitting a young girl like Mai over the head – I'm not having it!"

Chapter 12

"And B flat, E flat, C minor, strum!" Mark, the leader of the Super Ukers shouted out chord changes as the group practiced. Mrs. O'Brien could see Peadair with his Tenor ukulele, his face screwed up in concentration and the tip of his tongue sticking out, like a schoolboy at his studies. Clara was with the Soprano players, playing with gay abandon and a tad more style than accuracy. Catherine and Eamonn sat with the Concerts, and as seasoned players, encouraged the others to keep up.

"It's a mighty little instrument," Michael remarked. "I used to think it was a toy, but when you see some of these instruments – the exotic woods, the gloss finish – they're works of art. And the sound!"

"I love them," Teresa said simply. "Cathal used to complain all the time about them – taking up space from his precious violins – but they're so much fun, they can sound amazing, and they bring people together. Like this." She gestured to the rehearsing group, now segueing into an upbeat pop song, the lyrics urging everyone to be happy, and to clap along with the melody. "This is what music is all about. We can't all be concert performers. But we can all have a sing-along."

"Lisa said she's thinking of learning ukulele," Michael remarked. Teresa grinned, correctly identifying the young man's change of heart about the tiny instrument. "She says it's great for teaching musicianship. Did I tell you she's going to be teaching in the Academy?"

"Yes, you mentioned it. Once or twice. It's great news, a very prestigious post – and they're lucky to have her, to be fair." Lisa was easily one of the best classical violinists in Ireland, in her considered opinion and unlike some of her colleagues, she also played Irish Traditional Music, as well as Jazz, with the same talent.

"Are ye still meeting up on the weekend?"

"Yes, I'm picking her up for the picnic at two pm next Sunday. Which reminds me, do you have any cushions? Nice ones I mean. I meant to buy some this afternoon but with everything that happened I clean forgot."

"Cushions? I'm not sure…"

"You're the one said, go all out. Impress her. Rugs, cushions and so on."

"Oh. I did, didn't I. Okay. Remind me and I'll give you some nice ones." The Super Ukers reached a final, rousing crash of chords and cheered, echoed by the few people listening. "Come on, lets catch the others."

She managed to catch Clara's eye before the woman started chatting to her fellow players, calling her over with a wave of her hand. The others followed, faces alight with curiosity.

"Mrs. O'Brien, you finally came to a rehearsal! What did you think?"

"You're sounding great, it was most impressive. But I've some news for ye, bad news, and we need to have a think. Can I drag ye away from the rehearsal for a while?"

"Of course." Clara's habitual air of scatty disorganization

disappeared and in its stead was the quiet, authoritative air of a woman used to managing and leading. "There's a small room in here, come on."

Once the door had shut, and they were alone, Teresa began. "First of all, Mai has been hurt. Not too badly, and she'll be absolutely fine, but she got a bad fright."

She filled the others in quickly, describing how Denise had been called away and how Mai had gone to lock up for her. "Luckily, we got worried when she didn't come straight back." She explained about the security cameras in the noodle bar and how nothing untoward had shown up.

"How this attacker got in and out is a mystery," she finished up, "But not for long. I'm going to concentrate on that, and if we can figure it out, it may go a long way towards proving that someone other than Dan could have attacked Pollard."

"And surely what happened to Mai helps Dan too? If he was with Denise, then he couldn't have hurt Mai and it seems unlikely that two separate people are going around trying to bump off West Stephen Street shop keepers!"

"Why attack Mai at all?" Peadair had been ruminating quietly while the others exclaimed and discussed. "It seems mad to me, a huge risk. There has to be a reason for it, unless the Gardaí are right and it *was* just a burglary. It could be coincidence."

"I take your point, Peadair. Okay, then – why would the murderer risk returning to the café, and attacking a young girl?"

Everyone sat and considered this in silence for a while. Catherine was the first to offer a guess.

"They left something behind that could identify them?"

"Something the Gardaí and an experienced, top class forensics team missed?"

"Ah. Well, when you put it like that…okay then, not something they left behind from the murder but something they wanted from the building. Something we don't realize is there, but they need for some reason."

"I wish Mai was here to take notes," Clara said. "But I'll play secretary until she's back on her feet. Right – to retrieve or steal an item, as yet unknown."

"Well, how about this – the murderer thought killing Pollard was enough to derail the protests but now the WE SIT has reconvened, they are trying to scare off businesses through intimidation and violence?"

"It's hard to see how killing Pollard was in their interests, Eamonn – he was part of the attempt to drive out tenants, he was on the side of the developers. But maybe, attacking Mai *was* just to intimidate…"

"Let me write that one down. Random attack to stop tenants organizing. And if we all have our pet theories, let me add one. Mai asking around made them nervous. She said herself, she's been in and out of every shop and business in the area chatting about the murder, the developers, the tenants protesting. What if someone thought she'd found out something incriminating?"

Teresa nodded. "Well, we need to sit down with Mai and go over everything she picked up, every nugget of gossip, in case that's true. Clara, that's your job. I'll let you know if she's being kept in or allowed home, but you visit her and find out. Eamonn, you need to explore it from your angle – how does killing Pollard fit together with intimidating the tenants, regardless of whether or not the attack tonight is connected."

"Will do! I think it's worth considering."

"I'll get Ronan Mac Manus to introduce me to some of the planning board, and maybe a few other Councillors. I'll see if I can get a better handle on how Brook and Pollard Limited are linked into recent developments."

"Excellent. Catherine, I need your legal expertise." Teresa pointed at the young solicitor. "Can you find out for me if there have been any legal challenges to either Brook and Pollard Limited or Southside Developments in the last five years, or so?"

"Absolutely. Why, though?"

"Just something someone said...I want to know if anyone has been successful in protesting or suing them."

"I'll ask around about the protests," she volunteered. "And any legal issues and so forth. I'll have a chat with anyone I can find that has had dealings with them."

"We need any inside information they can give us. And I mean rumour, innuendo, scurrilous gossip too. Anything." It was one advantage of not being official investigators, she thought wryly. We don't have only consider hard, cold facts. Sometimes, a bit of tittle-tattle was just as valuable.

"And be careful, all of you. Don't take any chances, and don't make yourselves obvious. Whoever is behind this probably knows I'm sniffing around, Michael too – I'm hoping ye are not on his radar yet."

She felt utterly weary by the time they parted ways, but there was still work to be done. The comforts of home would have to wait – first she wanted to talk to Denise and Dan. Neither were answering their phone, and although she had texted asking Denise to ring her urgently, she hadn't liked to write baldly that Mai was hurt. It wasn't something you wanted to find out by text! But at this point she needed to get hold of them – and better to hear it from her than Detective Malachy Flynn tomorrow.

Ring me. Mai got hurt, closing up café.

She didn't have long to wait – Denise responded within seconds, her voice shaky – with fright or from some other cause, Teresa couldn't tell.

"Oh my god! What happened?"

"She's okay now, but while she was closing up, someone hit her over the head and left her lying there. Michael and I found her reasonably quickly, and she's in hospital now."

"That's my fault…But I never thought for a moment there was any danger, all she had to do was make sure everything was turned off, and set the alarm."

"You couldn't have known, Denise." Teresa tried to think of a way to put her next question tactfully. "I believe you met up with Dan – Mai said that's why she closed for you?"

"Oh." There was a distinct lack of enthusiasm in the reply. "I got a phone call from him, asking me to go visit him. It was a really bad line, but he said, "I need you to come to my mother's house, as soon as you can." Like, she lives out near Howth, Mrs. O'Brien." Howth was a lovely area, out on the far north coast of Dublin, a fishing village really but considered part of the city and linked to the city centre by a light railway known as the DART. "It's a long way to go, you know yourself. But I was dying to see him, so I trekked all the way out there only – he wasn't there!"

"What?" This was not good news.

"He wasn't there. His mother said he got a phone call, something urgent, and he left the house at a run. Said to tell me to wait, and he'd be back in half an hour. I sat in that woman's living room, drinking tea and making small talk about the flipping weather for almost an hour. It was humiliating Eventually he texted to say he had been delayed and that I might as well head home…"

"Oh dear. That is…well, it's very thoughtless of him. But he is under immense stress at the moment, dear. It's possible he simply couldn't help what happened, and he'll explain it all when you do manage to meet up…"

Or, a treacherous little voice whispered, it's possible that he lured Denise out of the café, to get in and hunt for something – something he couldn't look for with her there, something incriminating. Then he found Mai locking up, panicked and - but there her imagination failed her. The idea of Dan hitting Mai, a kid he'd known since she was six years of age, over the head and leaving her injured on the floor…no.

She was glad to note that Denise, while upset about her own disappointment, immediately returned to asking about Mai, and while a few weeks previously she would have been a teary mess, now righteous anger burned in its place. She rang off, anxious to contact the Khans and Teresa promised to let her know if she heard from them first.

Dan rang almost as soon as she said goodbye to Denise. He sounded dreadful, hoarse and frightened.

"Mai…Is she…Please tell me, is she okay?"

"She's fine. Well, not fine obviously, her head hurts and she had a terrible fright, but she's going to be grand."

"Oh thank heavens. I thought – well, you know yourself. Mrs. O'Brien, you can't help thinking the worst. What's happening to us? This is a nightmare. Why would anyone attack that poor kid? She's a dote, everyone loves her. None of this makes sense."

"I know, I know. But we will make sense of it, don't you worry. And on that note, what happened to you this afternoon?"

There was a pause. "What do you mean?"

"You asked Denise to go visit you. Then you bail on her, then you send her home…what are you playing at?"

"It's complicated. It's – oh, it'll sound unbelievable. What's the point? I keep telling everyone I didn't kill that man and no one believes it. And now they'll probably think I hurt Mai, which I would never do, but I have no alibi for that either now…"

"Dan Riordan. Pull yourself together man, and listen to me. No one believes you killed Pollard. Is that what you've been thinking? Is that why you're hiding yourself away? Well, let me tell you something, not only do we not believe it, there is an entire gang of people working hard to prove your innocence. Even Detective Garda Flynn isn't convinced you did it."

"But – the newspapers and the media – they said there were no other suspects. They had quotes from "Local Businesses" about how they were shocked at me, how I've a temper and- and all sorts."

"Oh, for – Honestly, do you think anyone who actually knows you would talk to journalists like that? It's a big story, the media will make four column inches out of the words "No comment!" We are all behind you, ya big numpty."

She ignored the sniffles from the other end of the phone. Anyone was entitled to a wee cry when they realized they weren't as alone as they had thought. But she cut it short with the words, "You need to tell me everything, Dan, from the beginning. What did happen this afternoon?"

He steadied himself, and when he answered, he sounded more like the old Dan.

"The thing is, I didn't ask Denise to come to Howth. She texted me saying she was on her way out to the house. You probably know I told her a few times to stay away. I didn't want her mixed up with me more than she already was. But when she said she was already en route – I missed her, to be honest. And also, my solicitor had said I should get the ownership of the café sorted, in case things went badly for me. So I thought why not? Might as well tackle it. Long story short, I was going to sign over my half to her, so she wouldn't be left high and dry. She doesn't deserve to be dragged into all this. I convinced myself to let her come. Which was great, but about twenty minutes later, our landline rang. It's usually for Mam, only her friends ring here like that, everyone rings me on my mobile. But I answered it for her, and a voice – it was very hard to hear properly, there was a lot of interference on the line – a voice asked if I was Dan Riordan, then said "If you want to hear something to your advantage, something about the murder, come to the pier. Now, alone!" and hung up. I know it sounds mad, telling it back to you, but at the time, all I could think of was maybe someone knew something that could clear me! I told Mam I had to go meet someone for business, and made her promise to ask Denise to wait."

So far, so good, Teresa thought. It was a bit far fetched but it fit in with several possible theories floating around her head.

"I drove to the pier in Howth Village – we're up on the hill, above it – and waited around the car park for a while. No one was there, only a few dog walkers and some young teens, hanging around. I started to walk along the pier, but no one approached me. I looked everywhere I could think of, and it's a long pier, but nothing happened. Then it started to rain, so I went back to the car, but – I couldn't bring myself to leave. I kept thinking, what if I miss my one chance to help myself? I got out of the car a few times and wandered around, hoping someone would come up to me…in the end I gave up. I texted Denise to go home." He sighed. "I bet she's raging with me."

"She's not impressed, no. If you had trusted her enough to tell her exactly what you were doing, then I think you'd have found her waiting for you, even if it took hours." She let that sink into his addled brain.

"As for your mysterious caller, someone also called Denise from a landline and pretended to be you. She thought you had invited her out to Howth. Then that someone decided to put you in an invidious position, while they took the opportunity to search your premises. But I think they miscalculated."

"Because they weren't expecting Mai to be there?"

"That too, but no – because between you walking around the car park, and making yourself conspicuous on the pier, I think you'll find you do have an alibi."

"Oh. You mean, people might remember me?"

"Were you wearing that red anorak you normally wear?"

"I was."

Teresa closed her eyes and visualized a tall, anxious looking man, in a bright red anorak making eye-contact with every passerby and their dog, wandering the length of the famous Howth pier and then hopping in and out of a car in the rain.

"Yes, I think I can almost guarantee someone will remember you."

Chapter 13

"The poor man," Clara sighed. "Imagine sitting out there in his Mam's house, all alone, thinking we all hated him!"

A hastily convened meeting had been called on the WhatsApp group, now labeled "The Super Sleuths," – its third name change, starting as "Music Murder Mystery" then morphing into "String Detectives" ("because we're all string players," Eamonn had argued.) Everyone was huddled over hot coffee and cakes in *Fancies*, as the rain pounded against the grey pavement and battered the window. Irish weather being nine-tenths some version of rain, everyone just threw on an extra layer of raincoats and braved the storm. The excitement when Teresa revealed that Denise had been inveigled away from the cafe, and that Dan had been similarly decoyed from his house, was definitely worth braving a bit of rain.

"And did anyone recognize Dan, from the pier?"

"Yes, at least two people - they said he was incredibly shifty, and they were sure he was up to no good." Teresa couldn't help but laugh. "The big eejit, in and out of his car in the rain, eyeing up everyone who passed him! Dempsey is still convinced he killed Pollard but at least he can't blame him for Mai being attacked."

Mai had been released from hospital after an overnight stay and was recuperating at home. Mrs. Khan had come to work, explaining that her husband was worse than useless at the moment, fussing over Mai "like a hen with one chick!"

"I'm better off in here," she explained. "Mai doesn't need two of us hovering over her, and if Amir takes the evening shift, then I can have a nice quiet night in with my girl."

Denise had already been to call on the teen, bearing flowers, chocolates, an outrageously expensive computer game that she knew the girl was dying to get and endless apologies for having inadvertently put her in danger.

"It's not your fault," even Mai's parents insisted.

"Denise, it was six o'clock in the evening, not half eleven at night. No one expects trouble at that hour. Now, stop apologizing and have some cake…"

"They're such lovely people," Clara added. "I went out to see her before coming here. You'll be glad to know she's already complaining that she isn't ill and should be allowed to come into town. She says she's definitely not well enough for school, however."

"The wee brat." Michael said affectionately.

"So, I went over everything that happened with her and here's her story. She says there were a few people – shoppers, mainly – on the street as she went across to Fancies. She says she saw a couple enter the music shop – you've accounted for them, Mrs. O'Brien – and a few were looking in the window of the gift shop. She thinks she saw a man enter the Bald Bear Barbers, and Paddy confirmed that for me."

"She went inside, leaving the shutters halfway down to discourage anyone from coming in. She turned out the lights in the back office, checked the back door, tidied away a few items that had been left out on the counter and then went to set the alarm, which is on a panel directly behind the till, behind the glass counter." Clara glanced at her notes. "That's all she remembers, except for the pain of something hitting her head. She was preoccupied, she said, rushing not to be late meeting ye. But she's pretty sure that no one came in the front door – there was enough daylight that a shadow falling across it would have alerted her."

"Did she hear anything?" Teresa asked.

"Not a thing, I did think of that. But she said one thing was odd. The back door downstairs was locked, and bolted, it looked perfectly normal. But Dan stores the boxes of Styrofoam takeaway coffee cups there, in that hallway. They're usually stacked neatly, four or five high. They were all over the place, she had to pick them up."

"That's weird," Denise said. "I would have sworn they were in their normal place when I left. We were busy, and it's possible one of the staff knocked them over – I'll ask."

"Do, just in case. Okay. That's great Clara. Anyone else?"

Peadair cleared his throat.

"Ah. I have some intel. And also, something that might help the protest campaign." He produced a battered notebook, spiral bound, and opened it, looking like a policeman in an old crime show, about to give evidence in the dock. Teresa bit her lip and carefully avoided making eye contact with Michael, whose eyes were dancing in his head with suppressed mirth.

"I was making inquiries of the council when – are you all right, Michael?"

"Ahem. Yes. Sorry, Peadair. Just a tickley cough."

"Right then. Yes, I was making inquiries and someone I spoke to asked if I had contacted DIBs – Dublin Initiative for

117

Business – and gave me a number of a chap in there. Fran Crowley, lovely man."

"DIBs are very good," Mrs. O'Brien remarked. "Only way to get anything done around here. They had the graffiti off my windows last year, less than twenty-four hours after it happened."

"We all rely on them," Denise agreed. "I never thought of contacting them about this."

"Ah, well, you should have. Fran says they'll happily talk to the council and find out what's happening with this development. They're all for small business, they don't want the area turned into a soulless high street. I gave him the details for WE SIT and he'll be in touch. But, more relevant to this investigation, let me consult my notebook – are you sure you're all right, Michael?- he had lots to say about Brook and Pollard. They're known to DIBs, a real thorn in their side but get this, he says he always found Pollard unpleasant to talk to, but more reasonable in some ways. Pollard backed down over another building, around the corner in Fade Street, when DIBs pointed out that they were contravening health and safety in their proposed changes to the structure. DIBs put the information to the council, as well, and the plans had to be redrawn. Brook kicked up an awful stink, whereas Pollard accepted it." He looked around, frowning. "I'm not sure what that tells us, but it felt relevant."

"You've good instincts, Peadair." Teresa replied. "Anything else?"

"Yes," He looked very smug, and made a show of checking his notes. "Fran says a girl who works for them as a street ambassador – you know, checking on the various businesses, asking if they need anything, helping tourists – was in the St.

Stephen Hotel the day before the murder. She was chatting to one of the bar staff, when a row broke out between two customers. She recognized them, the moment the news broke about the murder."

"Who?" Everyone asked in unison.

"Brook and Pollard. They were huddled in a corner, talking in low voices, and then it turned nasty. Both men were red in the face, and shouting, and the barman had to tell them to calm down or get out."

"This is very interesting, very interesting indeed."

"Well done, Peadair," Clara said proudly.

"Ah well, I got lucky. Now, Fran says the girl gave a statement to the Gardaí but he'll ask if she would mind popping into the music shop later and telling Mrs. O'Brien what happened – first hand, like. I thought one of us could talk to the bar man too? He doesn't know the chap's name but Amy – the street ambassador – might."

"When we know, I'll ask one of ye to do it."

"My contribution – not as good as yours, Peadair – but here we go." Catherine grinned at Mrs. O'Brien. "Now, luckily my boss is a very understanding man, so I spent this morning checking up on our favourite "commercial property specialists," in a legal sense. I found a couple of events – they were brought to court by commercial tenants in a property out in Blanchardstown, near the shopping centre. They were seeking an injunction against building work starting, until the issue of their leases could be settled in a separate case. The injunction was granted, their case regarding the leases was upheld and the planned development didn't go ahead. That was about five years ago. Incidentally that was the last time they seem to have been involved in any work outside the city centre. Blanchardstown comes under the county council, not the city council – they seem to have been less favourably inclined towards Brook and Pollard Limited."

"Now, the next thing I found was three years ago – A company called Leinster Holdings bought a building in Dame Street, gave the management contract to Brook and Pollard, who promptly tried to raise rents, intimidate tenants and make themselves unpleasant – six businesses on three floors and the tenants took them to court. That one was settled out of court, the tenants moved on, the building became a super-pub. One of those ugly, tourist traps with over-priced beer and noisy gaming machines. I found a few more like this – the pattern is the same each time. A company buys the building, Brook and Pollard make life miserable for the tenants, it goes to a certain point legally, the tenants give up and settle."

"That's what they were trying to do to us!" Denise exclaimed. "Only it didn't get as far as that, yet."

"I tracked down one of the tenants involved in the Dame Street case. She's still trading, but out of the city centre – Rathmines. Same name, though. She said, they were initially determined to go all the way with it, but it just got too much for them. Endless complaints about noise, tiny infractions reported to the council, harassed at every turn by the agents and she says she was scared when she realized how big their legal fees could get. What if they lost and had to pay costs? Also, she mentioned Seamus Molloy – said it seemed pointless to keep fighting when he had the rest of the council in his pocket, ready to support the development. Oh, except for Michelle Costello. She said, if it wasn't for her, they might not have got a settlement at all out of it."

Teresa stared at the younger woman, her minding whirring.

The others remained silent, watching her. Eventually she gave herself a little shake and said "Thanks, Catherine. I think I'm beginning to see something now. It's taking shape."

"Ooh!" Eamonn grinned. "Care to share?"

"Not yet…and what about you, Eamonn? Anything to add?"

"Sort of…Remember you said we should chase up everything – rumours, scandal and so on? Well, I did just that. Plus, I got some hard information from my hacker buddy to add to it. He's been doing a deep dive into the directors of this Southside Developments company. I won't bore you with the details, he had to follow a lot of trails to find the answers, but apart from Annmarie Pollard, none of them are legit. They're paid to sign off on company registrations. They get a lump sum payment, then an agreement is drawn up giving them a tiny percentage of shares in the company. The company usually only exists for a short period of time, it's dissolved before anyone can inquire too closely and then a new one is formed, for a new project. The company is above board as far as the revenue is concerned and it appears to comply to all the requirements for a limited company under Irish law – that's what makes it so clever. I'm not even sure it's illegal – Catherine says it's sailing close to the line, though."

"Do these people pop up on any other company?"

"Oh yes, but not with Brook and Pollard. But then we started looking at it from another angle – we looked at companies that owned the buildings Pollard would have managed. Each of those companies was formed in the same way – one member legitimately connected to the agents and the rest paid ringers. Catherine mentioned one there – Leinster Holdings. That one was fronted by a Damian Brook. Another one, fronted by a Carol Wilson, Brook's sister-in-law. These companies were essentially fronts for their firm. They buy up a building, pretend they're just the managing agents acting on instructions from their clients, and then they set about harassing the tenants."

"Surely, some of this is illegal?" Denise asked plaintively. "Tell me they can't get away with it?"

"It's extremely dodgy," Catherine replied, "But we need to tread carefully. There are a lot of loopholes that people exploit, perfectly legally. It does seem to me though, maybe it's not our problem. This is one for the Revenue Commission."

"Catherine, you're a genius!"

"I try," she smiled. "Seriously though, I very much doubt that if they went to those lengths to cover their tracks, everything is above board financially. And if the Revenue start digging, who knows where it will lead?"

"I'd love if it led to Councillor Molloy," Eamonn said sourly. "That man is as crooked as a corkscrew."

"He's certainly in the developers' camp, but that's not the same thing. I wonder – but anything we suspect, we have to prove and that's what we need to concentrate on now. Eamonn, you're our best bet for finding out as much as we can about these bogus companies, keep digging. The rest of you, follow up anything you can think of. And reach out to Dan, I've put his number in the group chat. He needs to know we're all behind him. Denise – would you ever just call out to the man, and be done with it? Even if you've to make small talk with his mother again?"

"I will. I promise."

Satisfied with the afternoon's work, Teresa turned her attentions back to the music shop. Today's clients included a visiting French orchestra who wanted to talk about the new generation strings coming on the market. New technology had advanced string making exponentially in recent years and Teresa prided herself on keeping up to date. A group of schoolkids trooped in, asking to look at ukuleles, and were quickly followed by a one mother, hassled and frazzled, who had been looking for them all over the shopping district.

"Honestly, I took my eyes off them for one minute and they disappeared. Only I have Jacyntha's phone on google maps, I would never have found them. Oh no, put that back. You're not buying a pink guitar."

"It's a ukulele, Mam," her daughter rolled her eyes and produced a fifty euro note. "It's great value, and I need one for school."

With one thing and another, the day flew by and thankfully, was followed by a nice, uneventful evening at home. For once, Mrs. O'Brien was able to relax and think about something other than murder and mayhem. Her mind wandered over the events on the news at six, the various customers that had been in and out, wondered how Finbar was getting on with recording his album, which reminded her of Michelle Costello and of course, ended back at murder and mayhem.

"So many different views of him," she thought sleepily. "So many different versions…"

She woke up early the following morning. Saturday was always her busiest day. She made breakfast, two slices of wholemeal toast and some marmalade followed by a yoghurt and brought it with her coffee out to the deck. The rain had given way overnight to a bright, and mild, September morning. The garden was lush and filled with early autumnal colours. She sat and thought of Cathal, working among the plants and rearranging her flowerbeds – often despite being asked not to! He had loved that garden. Marriage was a funny thing, she thought. You love each other, but it's always hard to live with another person, raise children together, do all the mundane things that have to be done in a household. You couldn't be unaware of each other's flaws. She supposed you chose to overlook them, or rather, weigh them up against the good and as long as the balance was on the positive side – abruptly, her thoughts swung to Annmarie Pollard. The widow had to have known what her husband was like, he even got her to sign up as a director to their shady company...

"I need to talk to her!" Teresa said it out loud, startling a friendly robin who was picking up the crumbs from her feet. But how to approach the woman? It wasn't as if she had an official role in the investigation. Maybe she could ask Detective Flynn to ask - but no! It would be second-hand information, filtered through the Garda's own bias. She needed to look into Annmarie Pollard's eyes, watch her body language...suddenly, as if he was sitting there beside her, she heard the gruff tones of her late husband, Cathal, repeating one of his favourite old sayings - "Truth stands where everything else fails."

"Let's try the straightforward approach," she thought, "and see where it gets us."

Chapter 14

If Clara was annoyed to be called at eight am on a Saturday morning, she hid it well. It took three calls in rapid succession to rouse her, which made Teresa feel a bit guilty, but she persevered until a sleepy voice answered the call.

"I'm sorry to disturb you, but I need the number for Joyce, from the Kitchen place."

"Wha'? Joyce's number?" Clara yawned, "Iz here somewhere. Peadair, Peadair, pass me my phone…not my phone, I'm on my phone, my glasses - ah, here we are." She called out the number. "What's going on? Are you looking for a kitchen?"

"No, you twit. I'm looking for Annmarie Pollard."

"Oh. Well, tell Joyce I say hi." Clara rang off, no doubt to resume her weekend lie-on.

The conversation with Joyce was short – Teresa explained briefly who she was, and that she was anxious to contact Annmarie. At first Joyce was understandably suspicious, although the mention of Clara's name did soften her. But she refused to hand over any contact details for her colleague.

"All I can do is pass on your details and it's up to her if she wants to contact you."

"I totally understand. If you could do that, I would be most grateful. It is very important, Joyce, I wouldn't bother you otherwise."

"That's okay. But I hope you understand, I can't give out someone's details without their permission."

Teresa did understand but she was still frustrated. It seemed urgent to her, to clear up this one point of confusion – who exactly was Liam Pollard?

"I don't understand," Michael said when she said as much to him later that morning. "We know who he was."

"We know a certain amount, yes. But we don't really know him."

He shrugged. "I'll take your word for it. Personally, he sounds like someone I wouldn't want to know better. Now, I need to lock myself in the workrooms, and get on with my repairs. Did you remember to bring in cushions for the picnic tomorrow?"

"They're in my car, along with a few other bits you might find useful."

She couldn't blame him for being more concerned about his big date, than the rather grim business of murder. The morning wore on, strangely slow in her opinion. A busy shop would generally make the day fly past, but until she heard from the widow, she couldn't settle in herself. She listened with half an ear to the customers' chatter and tried to look interested. The only bright spot was a visit from a dark-haired young woman with a gorgeous accent, who introduced herself as Amy from DIBs.

"Fran asked me to pop in," She spread her hands expressively. "I am not sure what I can do to help, but I'm happy to try."

"Could you describe what you saw and heard, the row between Brook and the man who died?"

Amy took a deep breath. "I've told the police, you know,

but I don't think they thought much of it. That gardeee, that Dempseeee, ah he wasn't at all interested and he hasn't asked me about it since. So yes, I think I can tell you too. There's a barman there, he is from Argentina, like me. My great grandmother Hilda was Irish, you know, from Longford. She married an Englishman and emigrated to Buenos Aires, way way back. And Mateo, he has an Irish grandmother, or great grandmother, I forget which. So we have much in common." She batted her long eyelashes and peeped at Teresa from under them. "He is a very nice, handsome boy. I like to call into him for a chat."

Teresa laughed. "Good for you. So, you were having a nice tête-à-tête with Mateo the day before the murder…"

"It is a very quiet lounge, in the St. Stephen hotel. Very respectable people. So when the two men started shouting, we all turned to look! The thin man, who looks like a rat, he kept shushing the other man, the one who died. That man was very angry, and he said, "You might as well tell me now, I'll find out." Then the other man- who was his business partner, I learn from the TV news - he put his hand on the arm and tried to pull his friend back into his seat. I thought for a moment they were going to come to blows! But Mateo shouted at them to calm down, or he would throw them out. The Pollard man stormed out. His friend just sat there looking angry, but he made no more trouble, so I forgot about him."

"You're sure that's what he said, though? That he would find out something?" Teresa asked.

"Absolutely. Mateo heard it too. But, like I said, the detective didn't care."

"Detective Dempsey. Yeah, I don't think he wants to hear anything that distracts from his pet theory," Teresa agreed.

"Amy, I can't thank you enough. This is very interesting."

The young woman took her leave, promising to call in another time to look at the instruments and chat. Teresa was soon caught up with another wave of customers, but her mind was definitely not fully on her business. As often happened when you wanted a quiet moment to think, everything that could go wrong, did so. The credit card machine broke down briefly, she couldn't put her hand to the new consignment of viola strings and had to search high and low while a customer waited impatiently and twice, she dropped the tape-gun on her foot while trying to wrap bubble wrap around a delicate violin bow.

Finally, having dealt with a particularly difficult woman who couldn't remember the name of the string her child required for their violin, nor the colour of the package, nor the colour binding on the string itself but was sure Mrs. O'Brien should remember her from three years previously, there was a ping and a message flashed up on her mobile's screen.

"Joyce gave me your number. This is Annmarie Pollard. What did you want to talk to me about?"

Teresa pursed her lips. It was a good sign that the woman had contacted her but the message was understandably wary. She thought hard about how to reply, eventually settling on -

"Thank you so much for contacting me. I know this is a bad time for you, and I sympathize deeply with your recent loss. But I do need to talk to you about your late husband. If you like, ask Detective Flynn who will vouch for me."

She signed it "Teresa O'Brien," and crossed her fingers. It took the other woman fifteen minutes to respond.

"Flynn says you're ok. I don't know what I can tell you, but if it gets some justice for Liam, I want to help. I will be in town shortly.

Can you meet me in the St. Stephen?"

"Yes!"

Teresa lost no time in responding, then told Michael to hold the fort while she was out. Michael preferred the safety of his workrooms to dealing with customers but he was more than capable of minding the shop in her absence and if he ran into difficulties, they'd just have to sort it out later. She wasn't about to miss her chance to interview Annmarie.

Looking around the lobby of the hotel, scouting out a nice table in a quiet spot, she felt an unaccustomed stab of nervousness. Used to being the queen of her little world, and confident in her role in the shop, or as a mother and grandmother, this experience was pulling her out of her comfort zone. She had been reared in an era with rules; be polite to your elders, be courteous, take responsibility, do your duty, don't discuss religion or politics with strangers and so on. Meeting a recently bereaved woman to whom she had never been introduced, and asking her questions about her murdered husband - there was no etiquette book in the world that covered that.

A handsome barman nodded in greeting, and she wandered over to the bar. He was dressed in the signature wine and black uniform of the St. Stephen Hotel with a name tag that read "Mateo." She smiled at him.

"Mateo, I just had a chat with a friend of yours. Amy."

The young man beamed at her. "Amy! How is she?"

"Very well, I think. I own the music shop at the bottom of the street, near the main road. She called in to me today and told me about the row you overheard, last week. Between the man who was murdered, in the cafe…"

"Ah yes," Mateo interrupted her eagerly. "Amy told me she

would talk to you."

"Could you tell me about it, if you have a moment?"

Mateo repeated what Amy had told her, not that she was surprised. The young woman had struck her as both a good observer and reliable. All Mateo could add to the account was that after Pollard had stomped out of the bar, Brook had remained at his seat for twenty minutes or so.

"I'm sorry, I didn't notice," he replied, when she asked what the man had done for that length of time. "I was busy. He passed me on the way out, that's how I know when he left."

"Never mind, Mateo. You and Amy have been a great help."

She took a seat, wondering if she'd be able to recognize Annmarie when she arrived. All she had to go on was a rather small photo on the staff page of Kitchen Magic's website. A waitress took her order for an Americano and Danish pastry, and she settled herself, trying to look calm and collected. The hotel door opened and a tall, blonde woman stepped in. She was slim and elegantly dressed, her tan Macintosh unbuttoned to reveal a crisp, white blouse and khaki linen trousers. From a distance she could easily pass for early thirties, despite the lack of makeup. As she approached the table, Teresa noted the dark circles under her eyes and the tense set of her jaw. Up close she looked a little older, but her blue eyes were gentle, and her smile was warm. The overall effect was of a very attractive, well-groomed person.

"Mrs. O'Brien?" The woman had a soft, well-bred voice. "I'm Annmarie Pollard."

"Please, call me Teresa. Thank you so much for coming to meet me, I do appreciate it. How did you know it was me?"

"I googled you," Annmarie said simply. "You're quite a well-known personality, in case you didn't know. I wanted to be sure I'd recognize you and - well, I wanted to be sure you were who you said you were, if you'll forgive me saying so."

"I understand, honestly. It must seem very odd, my contacting you like this."

"Not really. It was you, wasn't it? Who found my husband's - found Liam. In that cafe."

Teresa nodded. "Yes. It was. Michael - that's my colleague - and I were the first on the scene."

"I wanted to meet you anyway, at some point. He was - I can't bear to think of him, all alone. He would have hated that. Detective Flynn said it would have been very quick, almost instantaneous but - do you believe in an afterlife, Mrs. O'Brien?"

"Teresa, please. And yes, yes, I do. I don't think we know or understand quite what it is, or how it works, despite what religions say. But I think some things survive death. The spirit. Love. Definitely love. I think our loved ones care for us, from the other side."

Annmarie smiled. "Thank you. So do I. Detective Flynn said you and this Michael waited with the body, minded him. I think if he was still there, in spirit, he would have been comforted by that."

"Oh, my dear, it was the least we could do. He wasn't alone, not really, not for long."

"That does help to know, thank you. It's funny, I can't stop worrying about things like that, even though it doesn't make any difference really, does it?"

"What's happened to you is big, very big. Our minds shy away from the big things, and concentrate on odd little things, trying to break it all down into manageable pieces. I remember when my husband died, I was really worried that people would call for their instruments and they wouldn't be ready. I drove myself mad, thinking people would be calling to the shop while we were at the funeral. My daughter had to promise me that she would put a huge note on the door, beside the one saying, "Closed for Family Bereavement," saying, "Please note the workrooms are closed at present."" She chuckled. "It seems so trivial looking back."

"No, I totally understand. I bet you knew deep down, if he had been there, he would have worried about the instruments too. Am I right? Well then, you were worrying for him. Liam always fussed over the bin collection on a Monday morning. They collect before eight a.m., so if you forget to put the bins out the night before, it's a disaster. I woke up last Sunday at three in the morning and went outside, in my nightie, and dragged the wheelie bin to the curb. Blind panic, thinking I could have missed the collection. I wouldn't mind but the bin was half empty!"

Both women laughed, and by the time Annmarie had ordered and received her pot of tea and pastry, the ice was well and truly broken.

"While I am glad to have met you, Teresa, I gather there was something specific you wanted to talk to me about?"

"Ah. Yes. Well, this might sound a bit intrusive and you're well within your rights to tell me to mind my own business, but I wanted to ask you - what kind of man was your husband?"

Annmarie blinked. "Liam? What do you mean?"

"Wherever we go, whomever we talk to, we get a different view of him. Please don't be offended, but - well, people found him difficult. And it's hard to get a clear picture of some things. I spoke to a customer who said he was ruthless but straight. I spoke to a City Councillor who called him - I'm sorry to say -

crooked. One person tells us he sailed close to the wind, but always on the legal side and the next tells us he crossed the line regularly. It's hard to explain, but it's vital for me to know this - if we're to get anywhere close to finding out why he was killed - who exactly was Liam Pollard?"

The widow went so quiet, and still, Teresa was sure she had blown it. Any minute now, the woman would tell her where to shove her questions and understandably so. She held her breath.

"Liam," Annmarie said finally, "Liam was difficult to understand. When I first met him, I thought he was awful. Rude, money-grubbing, and unpleasant. He was involved in purchasing a building owned by my brother, and all I heard was how unreasonable he was, how hard a bargain he was driving...very off-putting. When I met him in the flesh, he seemed to be everything I had heard and more."

"Then, my brother died. Heart-attack, very suddenly. He was only forty years of age, and he had two small kids under five years of age. It was terrible. My sister-in-law went to pieces, and my parents weren't much better. Everything fell to me, including getting that building sold. Liam stopped bargaining - he offered full market price and paid up on the nose. It was such a relief. Then he told me that his firm was interested in another building my brother had owned. It was pretty small and in bad repair. I would have been glad to offload it for any amount, to be honest. Liam told me that there was a huge development planned and that if my sister-in-law held out for a few months, she'd get triple what was offered. I asked him why - why help us?"

"Do you know, he looked at me, quite offended, and said "It was different when your brother was alive. He knew what he was doing. It was a fair fight. It would be wrong to take advantage of his death." Right then, I realized there was more to him than met the eye."

She stared into the distance. "He grew on me after that. Yes, he was ruthless, and he found it hard to see the other person's point of view. He loved the fight - it didn't bother him if people resisted change or if they protested. He said it was their right and his right to push back and not give in. If they did something outside the terms of the lease, it was their own fault - as far as he was concerned, they broke the lease. But, if they won fair and square in court or if they proved he was wrong, well - then he walked away." She shrugged. "It might be hard to understand but in his own way, he was a very honourable man."

Teresa sat back and smiled. "If, for the sake of argument, Liam found out something - something his own side was doing, that was illegal rather than just hard business - what would he do?"

Annmarie frowned. "Ah. He would have confronted them - who are we talking about here? Brook? or the developers themselves? - Brook, he would have confronted. The clients -I think probably he would have just quietly withdrawn from the whole thing."

"Withdrawn? Wouldn't that have been difficult?"

"I don't think so - deals fall through all the time. There's no shortage of firms willing to take the work."

Teresa drew a deep breath. In for a penny, in for a pound, she thought.

"But - Annmarie, Southside Developments isn't just some client."

The widow looked at her blankly. "Isn't it? Why?"

If she was acting, she had missed her calling - she should have been accepting Oscars in Hollywood, not selling expensive kitchens in Dublin.

"Well, for a start, you're a director in that company. And the rest of the directors are …well, let's just say Southside belongs to your late husband's firm. It's a blind - a company they pretended was the landlord of the building in West Stephen Street. But it's their building really."

"That's - impossible."

"It's fact, Annmarie."

"It can't be." The woman spoke kindly but firmly. "You've got hold of the wrong end of the stick on this one. I've never been a director of a company, I think I would remember signing up for that!"

"Annmarie, you are listed as a director of Southside Holdings."

A frown creased her brow. "Teresa, I'm telling you -"

Teresa held up her phone, having first pulled up a screenshot of the paperwork for Southside that Eamonn had shared in the WhatsApp group.

"What is this? That's - oh my god…"

"I told you. I'm so sorry - I know this is the last thing you need right now. If it wasn't important, I wouldn't have told you."

"But - But I would have had to sign papers, and register and - how could someone make me a director without my knowledge?"

"I suppose Liam would have been able to set up an email for you, and intercept any letters…"

The widow narrowed her eyes and snapped, "Liam would never have done that. Never."

Teresa paused. "If not him, then who?"

"I don't know. I don't care what it looks like. Liam would not do that, I swear it." Her voice quivered with unshed tears, and she was as white as a sheet. "Please, you have to get to the bottom of this. If the Gardaí see this…"

"They'll have to know, Annmarie. They probably already do. But I promise you, I'll talk to Detective Flynn, make sure he knows you didn't sign up for it and I'll tell him you don't believe Liam knew either."

"Thank you. I'm sorry, I need to go now. I want to go home." She stood up, grabbed her bag and turned to go. As she walked away, she cast one last glance at Teresa and mustered a smile. "It's not your fault, don't worry. And I prefer to know, it would have been terrible to find out about it from the Gardaí. It's just been a shock."

"I understand, truly. I'm so sorry to have upset you. If you feel up to it, it would be nice to meet again for coffee sometime."

"Yes, I'd like that."

Teresa watched her go, feeling like a worm. Was any of this worth it, stirring up trouble for people? Perhaps she should just leave it to the professionals and stop being an interfering old woman.

Chapter 15

Michael Clancy grinned at Teresa, looking - as the late Cathal O'Brien would have said - like a man who had lost sixpence but found a pound.

"You remember Lisa," He gestured to the pretty brunette by his side. Lisa's smile was almost as wide as his.

"Good morning, Mrs. O'Brien."

Teresa bustled out from behind the counter and hugged the tall, slim girl.

"Of course I remember Lisa, ya mook." She winked at Lisa. "Michael here thinks I forget people as soon as the door closes on them. I'm old, not daft."

"You tell him," Lisa said. "Anyway, I just popped in to say hi to this fella and also check in with you. I would have been in earlier, but the orchestra was in Galway for the Festival and we only got back yesterday. Michael tells me you're up to your neck in another case." She looked at Teresa closely. "How are you holding up? It can't have been easy, finding that poor man like that."

"It wasn't. And to be honest, after today, I've a good mind to leave well enough alone. If it wasn't for Dan relying on me - well, I don't know if we're doing more harm than good."

The young couple insisted on hearing the whole story, Lisa

providing tea and cake from the cafe next door, and Michael promising to tend to any customers that might wander in early on a Saturday morning.

"Sit down now, and fill us in."

Teresa recounted her meeting with the widow. "I hurt the poor woman, not on purpose, but still - I wish I hadn't blundered in like that."

"Nonsense." Lisa shook her head and added, "She had to know, and better coming from you than Detective Flynn. Can you imagine what they would have made of it? Now she has a chance to contact her solicitor and hopefully prove it isn't her signature. And if you'll forgive me saying so, you can't abandon Denise and Dan just because the going got rough. If you hadn't solved the murder in the concert hall, what would have happened to me?"

Michael squeezed her arm. "It doesn't bear thinking about."

"So, while I'm terribly sorry for the poor woman, the best thing you can do for her is find her husband's killer."

Much comforted, Teresa munched a coffee slice - not quite as nice as her favourite honey cakes but a close runner - and sipped her coffee.

"I suppose so. And I did learn something from talking to her."

"There you go! Now, I have to run. Michael, I'll see you tomorrow for our picnic?"

"Absolutely. I'll walk you out…"

There was much whispering and giggling between the pair as they parted, and Teresa smiled to herself. Nothing like a bit of young love to brighten your day, she thought. All three of her children were married now, but the younger generation were getting to that age, when talk of weddings might be expected. She would enjoy a good wedding, and maybe if Michael got his act together, she wouldn't have to wait for her grand-kids to oblige. Her protegee came back inside whistling and flashed her a giant smile before he trotted up the stairs to his workroom.

Fortified and encouraged, she turned her thoughts to the mystery next door. Dan should be feeling a bit happier now he knew he had everyone's support. She could only hope that Denise had managed to see him, and maybe even Dan would realize what a loyal friend she was. But the problem of clearing his name still remained.

The victim was becoming clearer to her, but at the moment, that just complicated matters. There was still so much they didn't know, including how to fit the bits they did know together. She cast her mind back to the day of the murder - no one had seen anyone enter Fancies, and Denise hadn't passed anyone on her way to the St. Stephen. When Mai was attacked, the same problem - no one went in or out, and this time they had it on camera. That was the first thing they needed to solve.

Then there was this business with fake companies posing as the landlords for buildings secretly owned by Brook and Pollard. In one way she could see the advantage - you could deal with the tenants and blame the unseen, unknown fake landlords for everything. But it was quite a risk. The penalties for fraud - and fake directors, especially ones who didn't know their names were being used - were so steep, it hardly seemed worth it just to avoid some difficulties with tenants. No, there was more to it than that. She just didn't see it yet.

Where to start, she wondered.

Opening her chat in WhatsApp - now entitled "The Stephen Street Sleuths" thanks to Clara - She typed a message.

Annmarie didn't know her name was used for Southside, never signed anything. Swears Liam wouldn't have done it.

She had better inform Detective Flynn too, she thought guiltily, but she wanted to see what Eamonn and Catherine made of the information first.

Eamonn must have been sitting with his phone in hand, he replied so quickly.

"Mad stuff. Is she sure not her husband?"

"She's adamant. Says he simply wouldn't have done that to her."

"Okay. Leave it with me."

She was satisfied with that. It was only a matter of time before Eamonn, and his friend Sully, traced the source of the fake companies. Let them handle it.

"Thanks. Let me know soon as."

"Will do. We found interesting pattern - every building they owned was approved for planning permission, even ones who shouldn't have been. Listed building knocked down on the Green. "

Teresa hissed in surprise. Listed buildings, even grade two or three, were off the table. You might get permission to alter them, if you left the facade, but not demolish. Someone in power had to be in Brook's pocket, there was no other explanation. How could they have got away with destroying a part of Dublin's protected architecture without an inside man?

This was now her most urgent line of inquiry. It was time to find out more about the city politicians. She doubted there would be much point in talking to Seamus Molloy – everyone knew where he stood on knocking down Dublin's beautiful old architecture! – but while Michelle Costello had been quite low key at the meeting, she had a reputation for genuinely caring about preservation. What was needed was a more personal approach, Teresa decided. Informal, off the record, get the woman talking. She racked her brains for some way to meet her socially, and Finbar sprung to mind. He had remarked that she played regular traditional music gigs in her spare time; the famous mandolin player might know where Michelle would be likely to play that weekend.

She had known Finbar long enough to be on easy terms. He might appear on television and be showered with awards at home and abroad, but to her he would always be the scrawny, shy musician who got mandolin strings on credit when he was broke. Cathal O'Brien had listened to him playing, seated on a bockety old stool in the front of the shop, on a battered instrument that had seen better days. "That boy has it," Cathal had declared, and thereafter Finbar was one of the few exceptions to the "no money, no goods," rule.

He answered quickly, the sound of voices and a distant hum of traffic clearly audible in the background. "Howya, Mrs. O'Brien!"

"Good morning, Finbar, would you have a minute to talk?"

"For you, always. I'm just out with the wife, we're doing a bit of shopping in Grafton Street. Would you like me to call around?" He lowered his voice. "Please say yes, there's only so many dress shops I can take in one day!"

"In that case, yes, it's an emergency, and I'll need you for half an hour or so."

"You're a star!" He added loudly, "Oh dear! But of course I'll call round, you just hang on there and I will be as quick as I can!"

He hung up and Teresa settled in to wait. Sure enough, within ten minutes the door opened and Fintan bustled in, looking very well pleased with himself.

"I was never happier to hear from you," he said, "I love that woman dearly, but she can shop for Ireland. If shopping was an Olympic sport, she'd be a gold medalist. I have seen the inside of every dress shop in Dublin this morning, and she's tried on at least a dozen outfits in each. The eldest is getting married, you know, so she's obsessed with finding a mother of the bride costume."

"I thought that was next year?"

"It is. She says it doesn't do to leave these things to the last moment. Sure, it's just an excuse to visit all her favourite haunts and tell everyone about Mairead's wedding. *"She's wearing a blush pink dress with savor-de-offsky crystals"* or whatever they're called. Janey Mac! My brain almost melted out my ears."

"Now you know how she feels when you drag her around every music shop you can find."

"True, true. And I'm not complaining, mind. She deserves the bit of excitement. But I was delighted with the excuse to take a break. By the way, if she asks, you couldn't lift a heavy cello from a shelf in the stock room."

"And why didn't I call Michael to help?"

"He was out dossing, and didn't answer his phone," Finbar replied promptly.

"You're shameless! Poor Michael, what will Una think of him?"

"G'won out of that, sure don't all the women think he's just gorgeous? He can do no wrong in her eyes. Now, what can I help you with?"

"You know about the WE SIT protest? We're desperate to get a bit of traction with the council, especially the planning department. Michelle Costello came to our meeting, and she was helpful enough, but we need to get her really involved. If nothing else, we need to find out who else on the council might be sympathetic to us and who would be opposed. She has a reputation for caring about small businesses and being anti-developer - I just feel like she could be doing more to help us."

"She's a busy woman, by all accounts." There was a careful tone to his voice, and Teresa pricked up her ears. "Have you tried BIDS yet?"

"We have, and they were most helpful - but having an elected councilor on our side would be a game changer."

"Hmm. I suppose so. Look, she seems okay and I've heard she has helped a lot of small businesses fight back. It's just -" He looked a bit embarrassed. "Ah, it's my own personal prejudice, I suppose. She has a bit of a reputation among musicians, too. She's a good player, don't get me wrong, but she's an amateur. Not that that's a bad thing, some of the greatest Irish trad players have been amateurs, but she acts like a diva at gigs. Has to have the best seat, has to dictate the tempo, always criticizing other players."

"Ah. I understand, that would be very off-putting."

"I'm not egotistical, you know that. But I think I've earned the right to expect a little respect, especially from a younger player. She told me - *me!* - that my timing on "The Sandymount Reel" was off. I wouldn't have minded so much, only I wrote the blooming thing. She's arrogant, in my opinion."

"That's very bad behaviour, Finbar, and I quite understand why she's rubbed you up the wrong way. But..." Teresa searched for a diplomatic way to phrase it. "But that's not the point here. She might be a rude player, and maybe she's arrogant. It's immaterial if she is also willing to help us shut down this proposed development."

"You're right, of course. I'm sorry, it just rankled with me.

Of course, you should try to get her on board. Hopefully she can bring a few other politicians on board too."

"Exactly. Which brings me to my reason for calling you. You said she plays gigs most weekends in her spare time. Is there any chance you can find out where she would be playing this weekend?"

"I can do better than that. She will be playing in The Sally Gardens pub tonight, with her group. The Yoemen are supporting my lad's band."

Finbar's youngest son had followed his father into music but with a mixture of Irish folk and rock that was taking the charts by storm. "I can get you tickets, if you like. Costello's group is on first, and you can slip out before the young fella starts deafening everyone."

"I love his band," Teresa replied, "and you're fooling no one, we all know you're mad proud of him."

"Well then, how many tickets would you like? I'll say four, shall I? You can pick them up at the door."

Teresa thanked him and rewarded his helpfulness by taking out a very special instrument, one he had long admired. A Neapolitan, bowl backed mandolin from eighteen-ninety, made in Naples by Luigi Salzedo, a beauty of an instrument covered in tortoiseshell on the back and neck, each edge lined with silver fluting and mother-of-pearl embellishments on the fingerboard. His eyes lit up and he retreated happily to a corner of the shop to play away.

"When will you sell it to me, Mrs. O'Brien?" he asked as he took his leave.

"I can't, Finbar and you know it - all that tortoiseshell, it's not allowed anymore. But I will leave it to you in my will, I swear."

The pair had had this conversation many times before, and

although Finbar thought she was joking, he would one day be pleasantly surprised. Teresa had indeed left the instrument to him in her will.

Now there was a plan to get Michelle Costello more involved, Teresa needed a date for the evening. She thought about asking Michael, but he would be far better employed preparing a picnic for the lovely Lisa. On impulse, she rang Mrs. Khan and asked how Mai was doing.

"She's fine, thanks you for asking. She's actually back in school and back at work - she insisted. I'm surprised she hasn't been in to see you yet - although it's probably because her poor father won't let her out of his sight!"

"Ah, that's great news. I'll pop over and say hello. Before I do, would you be okay with me taking Mai out tonight? I have tickets for The Sally Gardens - a friend's son is playing there tonight with his band. I think she'd enjoy it." And by the sound of it, she thought, Mr. Khan could do with a night off from worrying about his irrepressible daughter.

"Oh, she'd love that. I'll text himself and let him know. What band is it? Would I have heard of them?"

"The Kings of Dublin. I know Lorcan O'Leary - well, I know his dad Finbar well."

There was a stunned silence at the other end of the call.

"The Kings of - Oh, my! I would go see them myself. A *fine* bunch of young men. Mai will be beside herself."

"Good, she deserves a treat."

"Go tell her, I'll square it with her dad."

Teresa took the earliest opportunity to slip across the road to the Noodle Palace. Mai was behind the counter, ladling freshly cooked noodles into large steel containers. Her face lit up when she spotted Teresa and she waved frantically.

"Oh my God, am I glad to see you! I tried to get over to the shop earlier but Dad growls like a Rottweiler every time I so much as twitch. He's in the office now, watching that stupid CCTV camera - it's his new hobby."

"I think you'll find he's on the phone to your mother," Teresa replied. "How would you like to come to a gig with me tonight?"

"Would I? Oh, my heavens, I'd literally do anything to get out of the house for a few hours!"

"So I gather. All going well, you'll be coming to The Sally Gardens with me -" Before she could finish the teenager started squealing.

"The Sally Gardens? The Kings of Dublin are playing there - are you for real? Please say you're not joking?"

"I'm dead serious. I have tickets -" The rest of her sentence was drowned out by the excited wail as Mai hugged her tightly.

"It won't be all pleasure," she warned the girl. "We're going to butter up Councillor Costello and get her more involved."

"I don't care. I'll be in the same room as Lorcan O'Leary. Wait until the girls at school hear about this - not even Phoebe Walsh could get tickets and her dad works in event management. Thank you, thank you!"

Mr. Khan emerged from the office, looking defeated. Mrs. Khan had obviously worked her magic.

"I suppose it'll be safe enough, Mai, if you really want to go?"

Mai grinned. "Wild horses couldn't stop me, Dad."

Chapter 16

In the end, Teresa recruited Catherine and Eamonn from the Super Ukers to accompany Mai and her to the gig. Clara had to regretfully decline, as she and Peadair had dinner plans, but the two young people jumped at the chance. When they arrived at the famous music venue, where generations of Irish musicians had made their debut, not only were there tickets waiting for them, but they were seated in the VIP area much to Mai's unbridled delight. She took half a dozen selfies showing their prime position in front of the stage, the plush seating, and the complementary bottle of champagne.

"This will shut Phoebe Walsh right up."

"Is this Phoebe your mortal enemy?" Eamonn asked archly.

Mai stared at him as if he had two heads. "No, she's a good mate. Why?"

Teresa and Catherine shared an amused look. Eamonn had a lot to learn about the vagaries of teenagers.

At eight o'clock, the lights dimmed, and an expectant hush fell over the crowd. A young girl, not much older than Mai, walked on stage carrying a set of Uilleann pipes. She kept her head down, as she sat and tucked the pipes under one arm. The last whispered conversations faded away as the first notes lilted into the air. A plaintive lament curled its way around the room, silencing even the clink and mutter of the bar area. The last note had hardly hit the air, but the player switched gears and launched into a toe-tapping jig that pulled the audience from melancholy to excitement, followed by a fast-paced reel. Spontaneous applause erupted as she finished her short set and she blushed deeply, almost running off the stage.

"What a talent!" Catherine exclaimed, "But so shy - the poor girl."

"She'll be fine," Teresa said. "If she could get up and play like that despite being shy, a bit of experience will give her confidence."

The next group was The Yoemen, named for the famed revolutionaries of Wexford - the home county of most of the ensemble. Teresa spotted Michelle immediately, indeed it was difficult to miss her. The politician took the centre chair of five, and moved it slightly forward, the others arranging themselves around her. She lifted her bow to the strings, holding it firmly along the bottom quarter of the stick in the traditional manner, and the others watched her closely. At a nod from her, they launched into a slick version of The Swallowtail jig followed by The Cliffs of Moher and the ever-popular Lark in the Morning. It was a very polished performance, a disciplined and accomplished group playing with a lot of energy and confidence.

It lacked the spellbinding magic of the lone Uilleann player, but there was no question about Michelle's talent. She was a very good player and led her group well.

Mai whispered to her, as the set ended, "She's very impressive."

"Yes. Did you enjoy it?"

"I loved the first girl - oh my goodness, imagine being able to play like that? And The Yoemen were very good just a bit - technical."

Teresa nodded. "I can see why she didn't go professional - assuming she wanted to. You need that extra something, a little special magic, it's the difference between being technically very good and being a true star."

The stage manager announced, *"a short break before the Kings of Dublin take the stage…"* and the lights went back to full strength. There was a mild stampede to the bar, but the VIP section was tended to by several lounge staff, offering table service. Mai was content with a diet soda, while the others ordered wine and beer. Catherine sipped her white wine and pulled a face.

"I never learn, wine is always horrible in this place. But I don't really drink beer or spirits."

Teresa grinned at her over her full pint. "My mother used to drink a pint of stout a day, lived to be ninety-nine. She'd have made a hundred, only she slipped on ice and broke her hip. You should try the black stuff."

"Ugh, no thanks. Oh - there she is." Catherine pointed with her glass. "Michelle, over there." The woman in question had just seated herself at a table in their section, flanked by two of her group on either side. Once again, it was clear who was in charge - they seemed to hang on her every word.

Teresa stood up and winked at her friends. "No time like the present." She made her way between the tables to where the Councillor was sitting.

"Michelle, that was an outstanding performance." She smiled down at the group. "I didn't know you played here, it was lovely to get to hear you finally."

"Oh. Thank you. Let me introduce you -" the woman gabbled off the names of her companions, Teresa nodding at each, knowing she hadn't a hope of remembering them.

"We all really enjoyed it," She slipped into an empty chair. "How long have you been playing together?"

Although she had addressed the group, they all looked at Michelle, who replied, "We formed the group about two years ago now. I played as a kid, but my real passion was climbing - I've tackled most of the great mountains around the world, at one time or another. But then I hurt my knee, and it wouldn't take long climbs anymore. That's when I went back to music. I used to play with a local group in Wexford but when I moved to Dublin, I found it hard to settle into it with strangers. So I advertised online, looking for musicians - and this lot turned up instead."

A polite titter greeted this last bit, Teresa felt sure it was Michelle's regular joke at their expense. No one seemed to take offense though.

"You play together so well, I would have thought it was longer than two years. How are you finding the fiddle?"

"The new strings are great, they've settled in well. If you have any more promotions on that brand, do let me know!"

"Of course. And you should drop the fiddle into Michael soon, let him tweak a little. He was saying he thought the soundpost could stand a little adjustment."

The talk turned to various problems that fiddlers encountered when playing in hot pubs, or under stage lights, and from that to the difficulties of working full time while trying to fit in rehearsals and gigs. Michelle would speak, and the others chimed in in agreement. Teresa was a good listener - years behind the counter had taught her to be quiet when someone wanted to talk. Before long the councilor was unloading about the trials and tribulations of being a city politician.

"Take today," Michelle said. "Three hours discussing whether or not a pair of gates could be removed to facilitate a cycle path. I wouldn't mind but the gates are never shut anyway! They're just a nuisance. But every little decision has to be trashed out endlessly. It's no wonder nothing gets done!"

Teresa took the opening that presented itself. "Well, a lot does get through though. How come so many developers get planning permission? Someone told me today about a listed building that was torn down to make way for a fashion outlet."

Michelle pursed her lips. "It does happen, sadly. And it shouldn't but we can't control every decision the planning board makes. I feel strongly about preserving our city but on the other hand, we also need progress. People want new business opportunities and jobs and so on. It's a struggle."

A very politic answer, but Teresa pushed a little harder.

"Ah yes, I agree and we can't keep the city like a museum. A listed building, though? Was there no investigation into how that happened."

The Councillor raised one eyebrow. "Investigation? There would have to be a serious complaint of wrongdoing, Mrs. O'Brien. Without knowing exactly what building is involved, I can't answer but look, if it was in disrepair, or there was a compelling need that superseded the fact the building is old…see, there could be perfectly legitimate reasons for the decision."

Teresa sighed. "I suppose so. Forgive me, I have developers on the brain. Watching my poor neighbours trying to get somewhere with this property firm - Southside - it's very upsetting."

Michelle clucked sympathetically. Her friends were chatting among themselves at this stage, and she glanced at them, before lowering her voice.

"Are they not having much luck, then?"

"No, not really. Oh, they're trying - organizing protests, contacting politicians and so forth. But it's hard to get any traction, especially in the media."

After the first flurry of articles following the protest meeting, it had proven hard to interest any journalist in the issue.

"What we need is a bit of guidance, from someone with experience."

"If you like, I can take a look at their plans - maybe I can suggest something the committee hasn't thought of. No promises, mind you. Have you approached the estate agents directly?"

"Brook and Pollard? Brook isn't interested in talking, Michelle."

"Ah. Look, I've a full plate at the moment but I'll see what I can do. Maybe I can arrange a press conference at the building, showcase the tenant's efforts. If you think it will help?"

"It would be a great help!" And it won't harm your image as a caring local politician either, Teresa thought. Still, it was a generous offer.

"Okay then, email me and remind me about it."

Teresa thanked her and took her leave, returning to her friends.

"Well?" Catherine asked, leaning forward eagerly.

"She's willing to help a bit more, said she could arrange a press conference to highlight the story."

"That's good news!" Mai said. "Now, hush - The Kings of Dublin are coming on."

Not another word could be exchanged during the main performance, a tour de force of traditional music layered with wild, almost punkish rock and punctuated by some haunting if very modern renditions of ballads and slow airs. Teresa thoroughly enjoyed it, but part of her mind was whirring away. She should have been satisfied with the evening's work - after all, helping the tenants was as important as solving the puzzle of Liam Pollard's death - but she was aware of an impasse in the investigation. She felt like she had all the pieces but no idea of how to put them together.

Eamonn and Catherine had to leave almost immediately, both pleading an early start for work in the morning. Teresa made sure to find and thank Finbar O'Leary for the tickets before taking Mai home. Much to the teenager's delight, the musician insisted they meet the band, and she left the venue loaded with band merchandise, a copy of their new album, and a hand that had actually touched the hands of the Kings of Dublin. She had a dazed look on her face and a smile that reached from ear to ear.

"Mrs. O'Brien, I love you. Seriously, if you ever need a favour, I owe you big time. This has been the best night of my life." She skipped into her house, singing.

As she drove home, Teresa felt tired.

"I'm not as young as I used to be," a treacherous little voice whispered. She shook her head. "I'm not done yet! Let's have another crack at Mr. Brook tomorrow. And I'll touch base with Detective Flynn. We're nearly there, I can feel it. "

Chapter 17

Just because it was Sunday, the investigation couldn't be allowed to stall.

Teresa had planned to ring Eugene Brook and pretend that she was still interested in selling. However, word of her involvement in the WE SIT protest had reached the surviving member of the firm and he gave her a curt, pointed rejection.

"I hardly think it's worth my while, considering you're trying to interfere in my client's business in the area." He hung up before she could reply.

Detective Flynn was a lot happier to hear from her.

"It's a rotten case," she could hear the weariness in his voice. "I don't mind telling you, it's not going the way you hoped. Your friend Dan is still the only realistic suspect we have."

"Have you a half hour to spare today? We have found out a few things, that might be of interest."

"For you, absolutely. Say, half eleven?" He named a cafe near her house, one that was famous locally for its Sunday brunch. "I could do with a bit of proper dinner, we've been pulling overtime all week."

Teresa walked the short distance to the cafe and was pleased to see it wasn't too packed. A table near the window afforded a pleasant view of the local park, but was secluded enough to

154

allow them to talk without fear of being overheard. Detective Flynn arrived promptly at half past eleven, looking dapper in a light tan pullover and khaki trousers. He looked tired, and his first order of business was to ask for a large coffee.

"I need to wake up a bit," He confided to Teresa. "I'm looking forward to a decent meal. They do a lovely Sunday roast here, although it's a bit early for it. I'll settle for the eggs Benedict, I think - with a few extras."

The few extras turned out to be sausages, two huge rashers and a grilled beef tomato. Teresa had the "full Irish," - a plate laden with rashers, sausages, eggs, black and white pudding - and a pot of strong Irish breakfast tea. "I rarely have a full cooked breakfast," she remarked, "But this will keep me going until dinner time."

"I skipped dinner yesterday, and the day before. I've been getting in late and out early. It's not good for the digestive system."

"Is it the case?"

"It is. I don't mind telling you, it's a nasty business. We're under pressure from the higher-ups to get it done. Your friend Dan is still the main - in fact, only - suspect. You will recall my young sidekick, Dempsey? He's hell bent on making the case against Dan. Ambition, Mrs. O'Brien, is a terrible thing."

"Please, call me Teresa. People make me feel so old, calling me Mrs. O'Brien all the time. I suppose Dempsey is right, looking from the outside…Dan looks like the obvious choice. But I can suggest a few others, if you're interested?"

"Am I interested? I'll buy you this fine brunch if you can shed a bit of light on all this. We have the politicians bleating about it, and lots of noise coming from various interest groups. Including, but not limited to, property developers, foreign investors and the media."

"I don't envy you. Would one of these politicians be the infamous Seamus Molloy?"

"Yes, but he's not the only one. He's only a local man, we have members of cabinet complaining - sure, half of them are landlords themselves! There's a sort of feeling that if we don't nip it in the bud, other tenants might get ideas about removing unscrupulous agents."

She chortled. "Back to the Land Wars of the nineteenth century, you mean? I don't think poor Dan makes a convincing revolutionary! He wouldn't know how to organize a small coffee morning, let alone a rebellion against the status quo. Have any other councillors been in touch?"

"Yes, a few of Molloy's sidekicks, and of course that Costello woman. She went over our heads, to the superintendent. Mind you, she was more concerned about the optics than anything. Worrying about how it would affect the development."

"Really?" Teresa wondered privately what Michelle Costello was hoping to achieve with that. As if he guessed her thoughts, Flynn added, "In fairness, she wasn't trying to pressure us, just curious as to whether or not it would affect the developer's plans. We couldn't answer of course, it's not within our remit. Passed her on to Pollard's partner, Brook. Not saying that weasel would give her the information though. You should ask Michelle what the outcome was. I'm sure your fellow rebels would like to know if the plans had been put on hold, or if Pollard's death had even slowed them down."

"Never mind that for now. Let me tell you what we've discovered." She explained about Brook and Pollard's record of creating fake - or at least, highly dodgy - companies to pose as landlords, for their own properties. "But it's only fair to tell you, his widow is adamant that Pollard would never have crossed that line. Especially, that he would not have forged her signature on a company director registration."

Flynn nodded. "That gives me something to work on, Teresa. I won't ask how you found that out - there are shortcuts a private person can take that we mere policemen can't - but now I know, it's a definite line of inquiry."

"My biggest problem is how someone could get into Fancies, without being seen. But we know now they did - the CCTV footage from Khan's shows no one entering the place after Denise locked up, but they got in somehow and attacked Mai."

"Hmm. Well now, let's go look at that, shall we?"

"What do you mean?"

"It's Sunday, the street will be quiet. I'm sure we could prevail on Denise to meet us there - it's about time we answered the question of how someone could gain entry."

Denise agreed eagerly, when Teresa rang to ask her. It was better, she said, than sitting fretting at home. Flynn was delighted; the generous brunch and hot coffee seemed to have revived the detective. He had a new spring in his step as he led Teresa to his car and the short drive into the city centre was whiled away with lively chatter.

Denise was waiting at the cafe for them and ushered them inside.

"Let me walk you through the place," she offered. "I know you've been over it before, but maybe we can bring fresh eyes to it? I've looked myself, and the others were here searching too, but we don't really even know what we are looking for."

"You'd be surprised how often a second or third look proves useful," Flynn agreed. "It's easy to overlook something, especially when you're used to the place. Lead on."

They made their way, through the ground floor, past the counter and the tiny office on the left and paused at the head of a flight of stairs.

"This leads downstairs to the rest of the seating area," Denise explained. They followed her down to the dark basement floor, waiting until she turned the light switches on before exploring the area.

Large couches lined the walls, with armchairs and bean bags in the centre, arranged around small low tables. A bookcase housed a selection of novels and history books, all set in or about Ireland, and all available to any guest to read. Another smaller set of shelves was home to board games and decks of cards. On the walls were framed photographs of the city, some in black and white and others in colour.

"They're very good," Flynn pointed at the art works.

"Dan." Denise replied, a ring of pride in her voice. "He has such a good eye with a camera, he could have been a professional."

She led them around a corner to a narrow corridor. "This is a storeroom," she indicated a small room with shelves filled with dry goods, napkins, tableware and other items necessary for a busy cafe. "And down here, at the end of this corridor is the back door."

Teresa stared at it, thinking of what Mai had told Clara - that the boxes of disposable coffee cups that were normally stored in front of the door had been scattered across the floor. "You moved the boxes that are usually kept here?"

Denise nodded. "Yes, we're trying to phase out disposable cups anyway and I got one of the lads to make room for them in the store. They were always in the way there, to be honest. We put the bins out there, and then have to get them back in -

I was forever moving the boxes."

"You have to bring the bins up the stairs?"

"No, we have a sort of dumb waiter that runs from the store room to the counter upstairs. You put the bin on it, press a button and it goes up."

"Can I see?"

Denise brought them into the storeroom.

"There - as you can see, it's just a sort of platform, which acts as a lift between the two floors." Denise placed a box of cutlery on the platform, which sat in an alcove about five feet in height. "It's plenty big enough for our bins, and we can run the heavy boxes up and down too." She pressed the button and the platform rose into the air, the box disappearing from sight. It was almost silent, Teresa noted.

"Let's have a look outside," she said.

The back door was heavy, reinforced with metal sheets and fastened with a large, old-fashioned lock and key.

"No bolts?" Flynn asked.

"No, we've always thought the lock was enough. And you can't get into the yard anyway, you'll see now." Denise pulled the door open, straining to hold it until she kicked a wooden doorstop against it to hold it in place. The trio stepped out into a small, cobbled courtyard, bordered on all four sides by the apartment building. Four stories of windows overlooked it, and the only door in or out was the back door of fancies.

Flynn sighed. "Well, it does seem to be a bit of a dead end."

"Hmm." Teresa was non-committal. "Come on, I want to look at the lane."

"Will I lock up?"

"No, Denise, if you don't mind. Stay here for me and keep this door open."

159

Teresa led the detective out to the front of the cafe and then ducked into the lane way that separated it from her own building. And archway linked the two buildings, across the entrance and the lane itself led down the side of the apartment block, widening out at the bottom, out of sight of the street. Here you could see the side and back of the building that housed Fancies, the back of a building that stood on the main street and the side-door of a pub that bordered both West Stephen Street and Aungier Street.

"Haven't been down here in years," Teresa said. "Not since these buildings went up. Did you know, years ago a church stood somewhere around here? Probably where the back of that building is. There was an old cemetery too, although it was cleared and moved a few decades ago."

"The city changes," Flynn replied. "But people stay the same."

Teresa smiled at him. "You're a man after my own heart, Detective. Now, tell me, see that door there - that leads into the apartments above Fancies, would you say?"

Flynn walked over to the door and pushed it open. "Unlocked!" He shook his head. "For the love of - they'll complain to us when they're burgled but you can't get people to keep these doors locked."

"I thought as much."

"You look pleased with yourself. Is it too much to hope you've a theory?"

"I have…ideas. No, not a solution - not yet. But I think I've figured a lot of it out. I have a few things to work out, yet."

"What's the plan of action?"

"I think it's time you met the others," Teresa conceded.

"Others?" Flynn looked slightly dubious. "Who are the others?"

"Well," said Teresa, pulling out her mobile and eyeing WhatsApp. "At the moment, they're calling themselves the "O'Brien's Task Force." You'll see soon enough."

Flynn rubbed his face and grinned. "In for a penny, in for a pound. They can only drum me off the force once, after all."

Chapter 18

Within an hour, everyone had gathered in *Fancies*.

Mai cleared her throat. "Hush, everyone. Detective Flynn can't hear ye when you all talk at once."

Malachy Flynn stared at the group. "Is this - is this everybody?"

"Yes, it's just Denise, Mai, Michael, Clara, Eamonn, Catherine and Peadair. Oh, and Setanta, too." Teresa smiled at the young student, who had decided to join them and as he put it, "*keep an eye on that eejit, Mai.*"

"Just the eight of ye, right." He rubbed his face with one hand. "I don't know why I'm surprised. You're like the Bow Street Irregulars, to Mrs. O'Brien's Sherlock Holmes."

"Oh!" Catherine whipped out her phone. "The West Stephen Street Irregulars...no, that's a bit long. Um - The O'Brien's Irregulars. I like that."

Teresa saw the look on the Garda's face. "The WhatsApp group," she explained. "They're still trying to settle on a name."

"Of course."

"Never mind that, Catherine. What about our reports?" Clara looked at Flynn eagerly. "I'm sure the good detective wants to hear about the case."

"I do, dear lady. I do."

"I'll go first." Catherine ignored Clara's look of chagrin and stood up. She looked as if she was addressing a courtroom, instead of a ragtag bunch of amateur investigators and one bemused garda. "I have searched every case, every hint of a lawsuit involving Brook and Pollard. There's more to that firm than any of us guessed. I don't know if you're aware, Detective Flynn, but Brook used to be in a different partnership. Between two thousand and nine and two thousand and fifteen, he was the junior partner in the firm of Moriarty and Brook. Moriarty seems to have been a legitimate estate agent, specializing in commercial sales and lets. Then he takes Brook on as a partner, and suddenly we see the same pattern emerging as now. A company is formed, solely to buy a particular property. Within a year, the tenants are removed, the property sold to developers, with Moriarty and Brook Limited acting as the agents."

She looked at Teresa. "Brook seems to have broken with Moriarty somewhere around February in twenty-fifteen. They were sued by the widow of a tenant who claimed they illegally evicted her and caused her husband to have a heart attack due to stress. It took a bit of digging, but I talked to someone involved in the case. There was no love lost between the pair by the end, and Moriarty openly blamed Brook - stopping just shy of calling him an out and out crook!"

Flynn whistled. "That is interesting. That implies Brook was at this long before he met Pollard."

"From what I can find out, he went into partnership with Pollard almost immediately. It's not surprising, they moved in similar circles and probably knew each other. Pollard must have been more amenable to his antics."

Teresa shook her head. "Moriarty, this first partner - from

what you've said, Brook went further than he intended?"

"Yes, that's the impression I was given. Like, he was happy enough to turn a blind eye until the whole mess blew up and he felt guilty."

Flynn smiled. "Ah, the cynicism of youth. Have you ever heard of Occam's razor? Never attribute to malice that which can be explained by stupidity."

"I see we're on the same page," Teresa remarked. The others looked confused, but she ignored the unspoken questions. Instead, she thanked Catherine, who yielded the floor - literally and figuratively - to Eamonn.

"I wish I had more to report," he said apologetically. "I asked Sully -um, my friend…a guy I know…"

"It's all right," Flynn said. "I won't ask how you found stuff out and I have a dreadful memory for names when it suits me."

"Okay, thanks. My friend is a genius at this sort of thing, so he has been digging around for us. He traced all the sham companies back to Brook and Pollard, and then went on digging, until he managed to contact a few of the people who were named as directors in them. He's had a bit of a past, Detective, so he knows people who know people, if you catch my drift. One of the people involved agreed to talk to him, and they said they were paid to put their name on the forms for the company registration. But he also claimed that he had never heard of Pollard before the murder hit the news. Brook was the one he dealt with, and he said Brook definitely had a partner but he was under the impression it was someone with a bit of clout, a mover and shaker. Said Brook boasted that no one would get into trouble, his partner would take care of it."

"Molloy!" Mai yelled. "I bet you anything, it's Seamus Molloy!"

"We don't know that, Mai. You can't go around accusing

people without proof."

"Ah, g'won out of that. He's as crooked as a corkscrew, and we all know it."

"Whoever it is, it explains how they've been getting away with things for so long." Clara said. "Although, I'm with Mai on this. I bet it's Molloy."

Teresa intervened. "Clara, you're up next."

"Mai and I have retraced every step she took, every conversation she had. To be honest, I doubt if there's anything she found out that would have presented a danger to the killer. All good, solid information, Mai - but nothing stood out that was worth attacking her for. So, we teamed up with Peadair, and started working on his idea." She addressed Detective Flynn, "We wondered if the killer had returned to the cafe to retrieve something. If they thought there was something in the place that would incriminate them, for example."

Flynn looked hopeful. "That would explain why they took such a risk, yes. How did you get on?"

"Um…" She looked crestfallen. "Not very well, to be honest. We looked around but - well, it's hard when you don't know what you're looking for."

"Where did you look?" Teresa asked.

"Under the sofas, and the counters," Peadair jumped in with the answer. "And in the storage room and so on. Denise helped."

"It was a long shot," Mai added. "But I really thought we might be on to something."

Teresa stood up and walked to the door. Without warning she turned off the lights, plunging the cafe into gloom and near darkness. It reminded Michael uncomfortably of the night they discovered Pollard's body.

"Don't turn that on!" Teresa said sharply, as Eamonn tried to get the torch on his phone to work. "Just wait."

She walked forward into the cafe, edging along the counter on the left and peering into the gloom. She leaned on the counter top with her arms and craned her neck, as if looking into the kitchen area, then swung around suddenly as if startled. Her hand slid along the counter, coming to rest against the first obstacle - the raised glass cabinet that was used to display one of each cake and delicacy on sale that day.

"Turn on the lights!" she instructed.

Mai sprung into action and the cafe was flooded with light.

"Help me lift this," She strained at the cabinet. Michael pushed her aside and lifted it several inches off the counter top.

"There!" Teresa said triumphantly pointing at a white envelope, thick with folded paper. Flynn produced a pair of latex gloves and a plastic bag from somewhere in his pockets and carefully retrieved the prize.

"What is it?"

"A vital piece of evidence," he said, "that needs to be processed properly." He smiled at their disappointed faces. "I promise, I'll let you know exactly what it is, as soon as I know myself. But this is good work, very good work indeed."

* * *

"It's not fair," Mai complained after Detective Flynn had hurried away, clutching the new evidence. "That was our find, not his."

"Mai, he's the Gardaí. Everything we find out has to been

turned over to him." Setanta said.

She pouted but let it go, turning instead to Teresa. "You were amazing. How on earth did you figure out where it was?"

"Logic. Pollard could only have been in the cafe a short time before he was attacked. Assuming he came to speak to Dan or Denise, rather than cause trouble, I just retraced his footsteps. He saw his attacker, because he was stabbed in the chest over there, so I guessed he might have been at the counter when disturbed by the killer. If he had anything on him, the easiest way to hide it was to slip it under the cabinet. Then he walked over to where he was attacked, trying to lead the person away from it."

The rest of the group stared at her.

"It makes sense when you say it," Mai said finally, "but I would never have thought of it."

"We searched the place and never thought of it," Peadair said. "Fat lot of use we were!"

"You were - all of you - of great use. You eliminated a lot of options, which made it much easier for me."

"Is that it then, do you think? Will the Gardaí examine the contents of the envelope and find out who the killer is?"

"That's a bit of an anti-climax," Eamonn grumbled. "I thought it would be like the books, you know. All the suspects in one place, and the detective accuses each on in turn. Instead, we'll probably find out by reading the papers like everyone else."

"Does it matter, if it clears Dan?" Denise asked. "As long as it proves it wasn't him, I don't care how we find out."

"Fair enough. Still, though - I would love to know what Pollard hid and why."

"It's getting late," Mai said. "I need to get going. Who wants to give me a lift?"

"I will," Setanta volunteered a shade too quickly, then tried to sound nonchalant. "Unless you need us, Mrs. O'Brien?"

"No, you run along. Mai, don't tell anyone about this. Same goes for all of you."

"I promise, I won't tell a soul. Setanta, you better shut that blabbermouth of yours too."

Setanta's indignant response followed Mai as she sashayed out the door.

"God help him," Peadair laughed, "He'll have his hands full with that young one."

"They squabble like siblings now, but give them a few years," Clara predicted. "I wouldn't be a bit surprised if they made a match of it."

"I suppose there's not much more we can do," Eamonn said, "Except wait to hear from the detective."

Teresa agreed with him and bade them all a good evening. Privately however, she was far from satisfied. There were lots of strands, all coming together...or rather, she mused, lots of notes that were beginning to make a coherent melody. She could almost hear it. There was the long history of crookedness involving Brook and his mysterious, powerful accomplice. There was the complicated character of Pollard, and his love for his wife Annmarie - possibly his only saving grace. Add in the obvious - the shady and greedy local politician, Seamus Molloy always in the pocket of developers and investors- and it should be simple. So why didn't it all fit together harmoniously?

She sat in her living room later that evening, feeling rather sad. It was at times like this she missed Cathal. He wasn't very interested in people, whereas she was fascinated by them, but he had a certain commonsense view of life that often cut straight to the heart of a matter. She would be waxing lyrical about a situation, positing theories on what had happened and why, and Cathal would look up from whatever book he had his nose stuck in and say one pithy remark that made her see things from a different perspective.

She glanced at his empty armchair, the match of hers, on the other side of the fireplace. "Well, Cathal, what would you make of it all?" she asked aloud.

He would probably be more interested in the state of Michelle Costello's fiddle, than in who killed Liam Pollard, if she was honest. The woman really did load the resin onto the bow, despite Michael's entreaties to be more sparing with it. Cathal would have been vexed by that. She was a funny one, that Councillor. Generous with her support and you had to admire her hard work to conserve the architecture of the city - despite limited success. It had to be hard, fighting the good fight against the likes of Seamus Molloy, knowing it would probably be in vain.

It might be interesting to talk to Molloy, she thought, if only to see if he was rattled when Brook's name popped up. It could be days before they heard from Flynn - she had only the vaguest idea what "processing evidence" meant in this instance - so why not continue to do a little gentle digging?

* * *

It was all very well to decide to meet a local Councillor, but a much harder proposition to actually achieve it. She rang his offices, only to be fobbed off by a polite but firm young woman, who said she would take the name and number and the Councillor would get back to her in due course. Teresa thanked her and left the information but didn't hold out much hope. A sneakier tactic was required, she felt.

It was a slow Monday morning in the music shop, which gave her time to search the internet. The terms "Local council events" coupled with his name yielded several articles from the social pages of newspapers and photographs of the politician with smiling dignitaries, celebrities and even a few ordinary voters. She added in that day's date, and a link entitled "Local Councillor to attend Academy Celebrations," popped up.

Clicking on it brought her to a picture of the Music Academy, and a few paragraphs detailing upcoming celebrations of the institute's centenary. A list of those attending included successful past pupils, celebrities and influential people. Added on was the line, "and several members of Dublin Council, including Cllr. Seamus Molloy…"

"Bingo!" Somewhere in her inbox was an invitation from the Academy to attend the event, an opportunity she had passed on to Michael and Lisa. She had felt strange about attending, without Cathal. It would be full of people who had grown up visiting his shop, buying their first instruments from him - he would have been in his element.

"Well, it looks like I'm going after all," She rolled her eyes. "Hope you're happy now!"

* * *

"I'm so glad you changed your mind," Lisa said, as they made their way into the Academy's auditorium and took their seats. "Michael too, he was delighted."

"I hope I'm not ruining your date," Teresa said with a twinkle. "I wouldn't want to be a third wheel."

"Don't be bold - but we had such a lovely date yesterday in the park, I think we can stand a little company tonight."

"It went well then?"

"Oh, it was perfect. Michael arranged a wonderful picnic - it was set out like something from a magazine or a film. We had cushions and rugs, and even though it was a bit chilly, it was perfect. Hot chocolate, coffee, buns, even tiny sandwiches with the crust cut off. He bribed Denise into making them, of course, but it's the thought that counts."

Teresa nodded. "He's serious about you, but you already know that."

"I'm serious about him too," Lisa said. "I was getting a bit worried, he was that long about declaring himself. Between us, if he hadn't said something soon, I was planning on doing it myself!"

"I take it I can refer to you as Michael's girlfriend, now?"

"You can," Lisa said smugly. "We are, as my mother says, an item."

"I am glad, my dear. For what it's worth you have my fullest approval."

"That means a lot, to both of us. Michael is fierce fond of you, you know. Now, tell me honestly. What's the agenda here?"

"Agenda?"

"Why did you suddenly decide to come tonight? Who are you hoping to meet?"

"You've a terrible suspicious mind. But you happen to be correct, so I'll forgive you. I want to meet Cllr. Molloy, see for myself who we're dealing with."

"Okay. I'll scout around and find someone who knows him. Sit tight! Michael will be here as soon as he parks the car."

The young violinist moved quickly through the line of seats

and was lost in the throng. Teresa amused herself with a little people watching, surprised at how many of the audience she recognized, even the younger celebrities. Her grandchildren were a great source of information on modern culture, she reflected. She was lost in trying to decide if the loud, blonde woman in a green sequined dress was in fact the lead singer of her grand-daughter's favourite group, The Banned, when Michael appeared, Lisa by his side. Behind Lisa, smiling and oozing easy charm, was the stout and flashily dressed figure of Councillor Seamus Molloy.

"Dear lady," He grasped both her hands in his. Luckily, she was sitting at the edge of a row of seats, or he would have seriously discommoded the people sitting in front of her. "When Lisa told me you were here, I had to come say hello!"

His accent was cultivated and middle-class but with a twang of something else underneath - a flatter, midlands note. "I knew your late husband quite well, wonderful man!"

To Teresa's absolute certainty, Cathal O'Brien had never clapped eyes on Molloy in his life and wouldn't have cared if he had. One had to make allowances for social conventions, she thought. He could hardly say that Lisa had dragged him over to meet her.

"Oh! That's very kind of you. Cathal was a great fan of yours, too." She offered up a silent prayer for forgiveness, a lie told in a good cause being no real lie at all. "Please do sit for a while."

Molloy lowered himself carefully into one of the rather spindly plastic seated chairs and wiped his face with a handkerchief. He looked rather flushed.

"Just for a moment, I have to get back to my wife. She's been cornered by that awful Costello woman - Michelle Costello, have you met her? You have? Ah well, then, you'll know what I mean. Drones on and on, and so sanctimonious. Do you know, she had the gall to have a go at me, in front of people, not ten minutes ago?"

Teresa assumed a look of sympathy. "How rude of her!"

Seamus nodded, pleased with the bit of attention. "Twenty years I've served this city, Mrs. O'Brien. There wouldn't be a parking zone nor half the streetlamps in the shopping district if it wasn't for me. I think I've earned the right not to be questioned by a jumped-up little guttersnipe like her!"

"But what possessed her, on an occasion like this?" Teresa clucked her tongue. "What could have been so important."

"Oh, she likes to pretend she's so concerned with local business, and preserving the city - she's a hypocrite, that's what she is."

"I've seen her at WE SIT protest meetings," she murmured, "I thought she was known for her work in stopping developers?"

"Ah. That's what she likes people to think. She's no angel, that's for sure." He looked genuinely upset, Teresa noted with surprise. "I'm at least honest about my opinions. I want jobs for this city. I want progress. And maybe that has to come at the expense of the old, and maybe it's not always fair to small businesses. But without foreign investment, the city will go back to the bad old days. You know what I'm talking about, don't you? High unemployment, tenement housing, kids leaving school at thirteen to do the work of a grown man - well, these young ones think money grows on trees. How do they think we can fund everything that needs doing without the larger companies, and department stores and so on?"

"There needs to be a balance, though," Teresa said gently. "Dublin is famous for its small shops, unique shops. We have to preserve the architecture too."

He sighed heavily. "It's true and despite what that woman would have people believe, I'm on the side of the small businesses too. I even went to that protest meeting - the night that poor man died. If there's a way to keep everyone happy, I'll find it."

Teresa stared at him. He was a very different animal to the sleek, fat cat she had been expecting. Michael and Lisa were pretending to be engrossed in the concert programme, but she knew that they were eavesdropping shamelessly. From the frown on both their faces, she knew she wasn't alone in feeling confused.

"Mr. Molloy, may I ask you - have you any reason, beyond her rather abrasive manner, for thinking Michelle Costello is - well, a hypocrite?"

The man puffed out his cheeks. "Beyond the fact that she pretends to care about the tenants being pushed out of West Stephen Street, but does nothing useful to help them? I mean, maybe it's just me but if my own cousin was the agent pressuring them to leave, I would have a word with him! Why won't she negotiate with him, and them such good friends?"

The look on her face must have given her inner thoughts away, because he paused and added, "You didn't know that? Sure, isn't her cousin Eugene Brook?"

Chapter 19

Mrs. O'Brien stood in the centre of her tiny retail section, on the customer side of the counter and waited. She had started her day early, sending out invitations to several people to meet her before she opened up for the day. Now, all she had to do was wait for them to arrive.

Detective Flynn had proved elusive, neither picking up her call nor responding to her texts but his colleague Detective Dempsey had reluctantly volunteered the information that he was in meetings that morning, with the Superintendent. "He'll get your messages, in due time," he had informed her, rather pompously. "I'll leave a note here for him as well."

"Detective Dempsey, I have every reason to believe the killer of Liam Pollard will be calling on me, before ten this morning. If you care to check with Detective Flynn, I think he'll want to know that." She could only hope a sense of urgency had penetrated the younger detective's stuffy attitude.

Michael and the Irregulars - Flynn's contribution to their nickname had stuck - were hiding in the back, although the level of stifled giggling and whispering made "hiding," a loose term. "Be quiet," she hissed, as a figure cast a shadow against the frosted glass. Her newly installed CCTV camera would catch the person's face; Setanta Kapoor had insisted on fitting a simple one early that morning. It sent the video to an app on his phone and no doubt he was watching closely from the back office. From her position however, all she could see was an outline. Was it whom she had thought?

Eugene Brook pushed open the door and stepped inside. He glanced around and nodded at Teresa but made no move towards her. Instead, he seemed to be waiting for something - or someone.

Another figure appeared. Slim, tall and dressed in a dark hoodie…she caught her breath as the hood dropped to reveal Councillor Michelle Costello.

"Good morning," the woman said, pleasantly, holding the door half open, and standing on the threshold. "You know Mr. Brook, I take it? He tells me you had him in here, valuing the building. It would have fetched a pretty penny, wouldn't it? Such a waste."

"Maybe her kids will be more amenable to selling, after she's gone!" Brook sneered. "I notice none of them opted to work with her, they're not interested in this place."

"No, they're not," Teresa agreed, matching Michelle's calm smile. "One is a doctor, one is an artist and the other is travelling the world. He's interested in climate change and conservationism, so he slow travels. Takes him ages but he seems to be enjoying himself. When the time comes, they all know my wishes."

"Hah! Well, you won't be around to know, will you." Michelle spun around, pulled the door shutter down, and slammed the door shut.

"What do you think you're doing, young lady?" Teresa asked sternly.

"I'm getting rid of a damn nuisance, that's what I'm doing.

Eugene, hold her arms."

"Me? No."

"Do as you're told, you sniveling fool."

"I've no gloves on me. I told you, this is your mess and you can clean it up."

"Her mess? Ah, so it wasn't your idea to remove your partner then?" Teresa leaned against the wooden counter. There wasn't a sound from the back now. "She really landed you in it, didn't she? Mind you, it was clever enough - to get a key to an empty apartment from you, drop out the window into the courtyard and then let herself in to Fancies through the back door. I think she probably used the dumb waiter to get upstairs so quietly - am I right, Michelle? - but at any rate she surprised Liam, just as he was about to talk to Dan."

She shook her head. "He wasn't a nice man, was he? But he was scrupulous enough in his own way. And he adored his wife. Using her name was a bad mistake - if he had discovered the rest, without that, he might well have been persuaded to keep quiet. Probably the end of your partnership, but he wouldn't have risked losing his share. The sight of Annmarie's forged signature though - that was too much for him. He went to the protest meeting, armed with proof that you were lying. The originals of the company registration documents, would be my guess."

"Shut up," Michelle's calm exterior cracked. "You think you're so clever, you interfering old cow! Did you think you could threaten us - without any consequences? The moment you sent that message, you left us with no choice. Eugene, for the love of - will you hold her steady?"

Eugene backed away, his face pale. "She knows everything, Michelle. What if she's told someone?"

"Who? That gormless twit who works for her or that stupid kid? Who's going to listen to them?"

"I might have told Detective Flynn," Teresa said helpfully. "Or the Super Ukers."

"The who? What are you babbling about?"

"There could be seven - no, eight - people in the back there, listening to every word. Recording you. In fact, if Mai - that "stupid kid" - is there, she's probably live streaming it right now."

Brook took a step back towards the counter and peered into the darkened room behind. "I can't see anyone."

"Of course you can't," scoffed Michelle. "The old fool is trying to bluff. Enough of this." She produced a long, slim bladed knife from her pocket. "Open the till, grab the cash. It'll look like a robbery gone wrong."

"Eugene Brook, if you put one hand on my cash desk, I'll break every finger on it." Teresa scowled at the man. He responded by retreating to the door and cowering.

Michelle screamed in frustration. "Eugene, you're a useless eejit. Fine then, I'll do it myself. I always have to, in the end." She raised the blade in a sweeping arc, ready to plunge it into Teresa - and screamed again as a strong hand grabbed her wrist and twisted it. Michael had vaulted the counter in the time it took her to take aim, and he pinned her to the floor with ease, kicking the knife away with his foot. Eugene Brook was struggling in the grip of Setanta Kapoor and Peadair Walsh. Long days on a GAA hurling pitch had given Setanta muscles of steel and Peadair had once been the star of the University wrestling team. Brook soon gave up trying to escape.

A thunderous banging on the door jolted everyone to their senses. Mai reached it first, unclipping it to admit a near frantic

Detective Flynn followed by a chastened looking Dempsey and several burly unformed Gardaí.

"I'd ask what was going on," Flynn said with asperity, "If it wasn't obvious. Mrs. O'Brien, if you had put yourself in harm's way, I'd have strangled you myself."

"I was never in any danger, Malachy," Teresa said serenely. "Mai, did you get all that?"

"Did she get it? She had me on a video call the whole time. We heard - and saw - everything."

"Well, then. I suggest you arrest this pair for the murder of Liam Pollard. And the assault on Mai Khan, and for being a pair of corrupt, greedy wastes of space."

* * *

"Coffee, and a honey cake," Dan placed them in front of Teresa, and sat down beside Denise. He reached for her hand and pressed it to his chest, making Denise turn pink with delight. Teresa smiled at the pair.

"I don't know what I would have done without you, both of you. It was like a nightmare. I couldn't prove I didn't do it and no one else seemed to have any motive. How on earth did you figure it all out?"

"I had a lot of help," she gestured to the Irregulars, which now officially included Setanta. He had even been added to the WhatsApp group. "It was a group effort."

"Ah here," Eamonn protested. "We might have found stuff out, but none of us had the first clue how to make it all fit."

"That was my contribution," Teresa said modestly. "It started with Pollard himself. On the surface he seemed such a thoroughly unpleasant piece of work but then there was his

179

wife. According to those who knew her, she is a decent woman and she loved him. Finbar O'Leary said he was tough but fair in his own way. So did Annmarie - she said if it was a fair fight, he was ruthless but if it wasn't, he was unexpectedly compassionate. Then there was the history of these sham companies...Brook was at it long before he teamed up with Pollard. He had an earlier partner, who got out once he realized just how far Brook was prepared to bend the law. I just couldn't believe that Pollard would allow Annmarie to get involved or worse, allow her signature to be forged. So, once I accepted that, I had to look at everything from another perspective."

"From the beginning, Michelle paid lip service to the idea of fighting the development. She pointed the finger at Molloy, and we all bought it. But when push came to shove, her advice was more about how to negotiate some compensation from the landlords than how to actually fight their corner. It didn't ring true to me. But she was so universally regarded as the champion of conservation and tenants' rights, I couldn't be sure she was Brook's long-term, secret business partner. The only thing to do was to examine the other, logical suspect. And Seamus Molloy turned out to be very different from what I was expecting."

"Michelle overplayed her hand yesterday evening. She saw me there and decided to cement her reputation for being anti-developer by having a go at Molloy in public. He was mortified, and angry enough to forget his usual suave political manner. He blurted out his dislike of the woman, and her relationship with Brook. Up til then, he thought it was beneath him to comment but she pushed him too far."

"How did you figure out her way into the building?" Clara asked.

"It was simple, when you look at it logically. Someone got in, and attacked Mai, without going in through the main entrance. It was reasonable to assume that they entered the same way as they did the night of the murder. The only clue was the figure slipping down the lane way. The only possible way in or out was through the back door - hence the boxes knocked over, when Mai went to lock up - and the only way into the courtyard is through that door or by jumping down from a ground floor apartment window. I asked myself, who had a key to all the apartments? The landlord, of course. I couldn't see Brook scrabbling through a window and clambering back up again, but Michelle told me herself she used to be a climber. She injured herself badly enough to give up hard climbs, but a small one would be child's play. She was willing to kill to stop Pollard exposing her. And she must have known if Brook was under investigation, he would give her up to save his own skin. Remember the phone call Pollard was overheard making, Mai? I think that was him telling Brook the jig was up. And then Amy and Mateo confirmed that the two men had met the day before the murder and had argued. "I'll find out" Pollard said. He threatened Brook, and then he went searching for proof to back up his suspicions. When he found it, it was worse than he had feared, and he decided to help the tenants expose his partner. He had to wait until the cafe closed to the public before he went over to tell Dan and Denise everything. Unfortunately for him, Michelle had already formulated her plan, and was ready to strike. And that's really all there was to it."

She sat back, took a sip of coffee and a large bite of honey cake.

"Was it her that got me out of the house, when Denise came to visit?"

"She couldn't resist over playing her hand," Teresa replied.

"She tricked Denise into going to visit you, and if she had left it at that, it would have been wiser. But she just had to over-complicate matters, and taunt you. I think she is a very cruel woman, you know. It amused her to watch people fighting for their homes and livelihoods, while knowing it was a foregone conclusion that they would lose. She would encourage them to take a measly amount of compensation and count themselves lucky. A very cruel woman."

She patted Dan's arm. "She'll have plenty of time now to regret her actions, at any rate."

"Mrs. O'Brien, you're a wonder." Dan said. "I'll never be able to thank you, but you'll have free coffee and cakes for the rest of time!"

* * *

Later that day a phone call from Detective Flynn confirmed Teresa's guess.

"The document was indeed the original paperwork. Brook was careless and left it in his filing cabinet in the office. Pollard must have suspected something. Brook confirms that he asked a lot of questions and was getting difficult. He must have decided to go dig around in his partner's papers after that row in the hotel bar. Imagine his shock when he found out that not only was Southside a sham company, but his own wife was implicated. He recognized the signature as a forgery immediately, of course. I think he took the papers with him and was about to give your WE SIT protest a whole barrel of ammunition."

Teresa passed on the information to Annmarie. The widow

was relieved, not only that her husband's killers were caught but that Liam had been exactly the man she believed him to be.

"Thank you, Teresa, I'll never forget this. You haven't just cleared your friend's name, you've given Liam back his too. I couldn't have borne it if his reputation had been tarnished like that, everyone believing he and I had been involved."

"No one will think that now," Teresa promised. "Michelle eventually confessed but even if she hadn't, between her confession and threats to me and the fact that Brook has turned over all the evidence necessary to convict them both, she's going away for everything. He really has no backbone, you know. She at least put up a fight."

"I hope they throw away the key, for them both," Annmarie said grimly. "I won't rest until I know they're behind bars."

"It's going to happen," Teresa said. "And when it does, a lot of people will get some measure of justice. She did a lot of harm to innocent folk over the years."

"Speaking of justice!" The widow's tone brightened. "My solicitor has informed me that I will almost certainly end up with the ownership of the building. That weasel was careful to put it through the business, so he could lay the blame at Liam's door if necessary. So now, with him in prison, I stand to inherit all the firm's assets."

"That's wonderful news, I am glad for you."

"It's not just good news for me. You can tell the tenants of West Stephen Street that there'll be no more talk of evictions! I'm going to be their landlord and they have nothing to worry about, I'll make everything right."

This news was conveyed to her fellow committee members as quickly as possible - by text and email - and greeted with universal joy. She left the owners of *Fancies* to last, wanting to see their faces in person. She called in as soon as she could get away from her customers, waited until the pair were free to chat and told them the news with a happy smile.

At first they just stared at her, unable to take it in. Then Denise sat down abruptly in a corner and indulged in a good, heartfelt cry.

Dan stared at her, then at Mrs. O'Brien, then ran to the crying woman with his arms outstretched. She saw him enfold her in an embrace, saying over and over, "Oh, my love, please don't cry!" - then she retreated to a discreet distance and pretended to be interested in that day's specials. She heard a group of tourists ask each other, "Should we ask if they're okay?" and shook her head at them.

"They're absolutely fine," she said. "Give them a minute. It's not every day a man realizes he's been in love with his business partner for years."

* * *

The O'Brien Irregulars gathered for a celebratory meal of noodles and coffee, crowded into the tiny shop, sitting on the counter, on an eclectic mix of stools and office chairs and in Mai's case, an upturned crate that had once housed a consignment of handmade bodhráns. The food had been supplied by the Khans and the coffee, with a box of luscious cakes, by Daniel and Denise. Teresa looked at the group, her eyes soft with affection.

"I can't believe it's over," Clara complained. "Peadair and I won't know what to do with ourselves. Although, I suppose we got a nice new kitchen out of it at least."

"I know what you mean," Catherine admitted. "It was really

exciting, being part of all this. Thanks, Mrs. O'Brien."

"I do wish you would all call me Teresa," she said.

"Can I call you Teresa, too?" Mai asked hopefully.

"No, your mother would skin you. Mrs. O'Brien to you, until you're eighteen." She burst out laughing at the teenager's deflated expression. "I'm joking, ya gom. Of course you can call me Teresa."

"Oh! Thanks, Mrs. O'Brien."

Everyone laughed and Peadair stood. "A toast…to our glorious leader, and the sharpest mind in Ireland. Teresa O'Brien!" To her horror, every single one of them stood and chorused, "Teresa O'Brien!"

She could feel her cheeks grow hot and red and hid her embarrassment with a gruff "Hush now," but the others just clapped and cheered all the harder. Lisa and Michael, Clara and Peadair, Eamonn and Catherine, Mai and Setanta, all united in admiration of the redoubtable old woman.

"Settle down. I must admit, it's been lovely to get to know you all better, and I hope we are all going to keep in touch…but it's true. It's over and hopefully none of us will ever have to think about murder again." Teresa spoke with finality.

Michael growled softly. "I knew there was something wrong with her, that Michelle one. It was the way she treated her fiddle. No respect."

The last word went to Mai, though. She gurgled with laughter.

"We should have seen she was the obvious suspect! Sure, wasn't she "on the fiddle" all the time?"

THE END

About the Author

Geraldine lives in Dublin, Ireland with her husband, two boys and her mother. Her work is mainly set in Ireland, especially in her beloved Dublin. A lot of her work draws on Irish heritage and society, and in her spare time she teaches Irish mythology, folk lore, and folk magic.

She studied in UCD, worked in Advertising and Publishing and finally returned to her family roots to run a famous music shop in Dublin. She retired in 2021 to devote herself full time to writing and teaching.

Her detective novels include modern mystery novels **The Body Politic** and **The Body Count** (*Caroline Jordan Mystery Series*) She also writes **The Old Bat Chronicles** as Nina Hayes: check out **The Kimberley Killing,** a cosy with a dollop of Irish magic.

She is proud to bring authentic Irish stories to life.

She has a very large and beautiful yarn collection and she loves to hear from readers.

You can connect with me on:

- http://www.celebratingwords.com
- https://twitter.com/gercelt
- https://www.facebook.com/geraldinemoorkensbyrne
- https://bio.link/germoorkensbyrne

Subscribe to my newsletter:

- https://mailchi.mp/a3703e884df5/author-sign-up

Also by Geraldine Moorkens Byrne

The Body Politic

Caroline Jordan is the rising star of Irish PR, juggling socialites, celebs and politicians. When her most important client is found dead at his desk, she's worried about her career - but if Minister Fitzpatrick was murdered, she has a lot more to be concerned about! Can she bag a new VIP client, romance the luscious Rory, and save her tiny PR firm - or will she fall prey to a ruthless murder stalking the corridors of power?

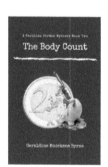

The Body Count

Jordan Pr is about to pitch for its biggest contract yet - helping the beleaguered Bank of Leinster recover public trust. The only problem is the fresh corpse in the meeting room...

This time Caroline is determined not to get involved, especially if it means dealing with DS Doyle and the Special Crimes Squad. But old crimes cast long shadows and in Ireland, no secret stays buried for long. Can Caroline possibly resist investigating the rising Body Count?

The Kimberly Killing

The Old Bat Chronicles Book 1.
  Writing as Nina Hayes.

Artist Eve Caulton is 50, divorced and ready for a new life. She can't believe her luck when she manages to buy Kimberly Cottage. She can look forward to peace and quiet, in one of Dublin's most exclusive suburbs.

But before she has even unpacked, there is a dead body in her living room and she's a chief suspect! Her mother Niamh calls on her gang of feisty older ladies, who bring wisdom, experience, and *very* special skills to the case. They might be known as "Old Bats" by some, but they will stop at nothing to untangle the secrets of Kimberly Cottage's past and solve the case before it's too late.

Murder and mischief with a dollop of Irish magic make this a fun, escapist cozy mystery!

Milton Keynes UK
Ingram Content Group UK Ltd.
UKHW010013290823
427665UK00001B/17